Elephant War
A Mac Williams Series
Book 2

Linda Robinson

ELEPHANT WAR

Copyright © 2024 by Linda Robinson. All rights reserved.

No part of this publication may be reproduced, distributed, or transmitted in any form or by any means, including photocopying, recording, or other electronic or mechanical methods, or by any information storage and retrieval system without the prior written permission of the rights holder, except in the case of very brief quotations embodied in critical reviews and certain other noncommercial uses permitted by copyright law.

This book is a work of fiction. The names, characters, places, and events are either the products of the author's imagination or are used fictitiously. Any resemblance to actual events, business establishments, locales, of persons, living or dead, is entirely coincidental.

Dedicated to Mom and Dad

ELEPHANT WAR

Cover illustration by the author

Chapter 1: The Golden Dragon

On the docks of the Port of Qingdao in China, a truck rolled up with a rattle and grind of gears, a sound that meant payday to Lin Chen. Steam rose from his breath, cutting through the chilly air. Scents of burlap, dirt, and musk assaulted his nose, unpleasant but par for the course. Large white bags filled the back of the truck. *This is the best haul yet*, Chen thought. His fingers shook from the cold as he took a long drag from his cigarette. It gave a satisfying sizzle, as he sucked it to the filter, then flicked it past his heavies, Bai and Jiang.

The dark-skinned man who had driven the truck stood and stared at him with an emotionless face and eyes that reflected hardship. Chen didn't know his name. The only information he had was that a Kenyan in a truck would be there at 1:00 a.m. His name wasn't important. None of their names were.

Bai pulled one of the bags from the truck. He was a brick wall in a suit. If Bai blocked a door, no one was getting through, which was why Chen employed him. He set the bag down, then pulled on the thick twine that opened it and inspected the contents. Seeming satisfied, he gave Chen a nod.

Chen walked over and reached into the bag. He scooped up a handful of pale grey pangolin scales, careful not to be cut by their sharp edges. They felt like thin rocks and sounded like poker chips, as he let them fall back into the bag.

Chen asked, "How much?"

"Five tons," the Kenyan answered, crossing his arms and raising his chin.

"Good, good." Chen motioned to Bai and Jiang to unload the rest. Jiang didn't have half the stature of Bai and was physically his opposite. What Bai had in brute force, Jiang had in intelligence, speed, and weapon skills.

Chen flashed an envelope, "The fifteen million rand as was agreed."

The Kenyan frowned. "You can get much more for them on the market."

Chen raised his eyebrows and addressed Jiang, "Did this man just accuse me of not being fair?"

Jiang smiled, "It would seem so, Mr. Lin." He opened his hands and closed them into fists, then he opened them again, stretching his fingers wide before letting them hang normally. Chen recognized Jiang's tell. It was something he always did if he believed there may be action.

"I'm paying you a good price for an animal that you can basically pick up without a chase," Chen spat at the Kenyan.

Stone faced, the man replied, "Maybe if your country didn't kill all yours, you wouldn't need the ones from Africa."

"Oh, we have a smart one." Chen looked at Jiang and Bai.

"Why don't you drive your truck around and see if you can get more money for your scales," Chen taunted, making a show of putting the envelope back in his jacket.

The Kenyan scowled.

Chen took out another cigarette from a silver holder. "You're new, and I can see maybe a little smarter than some." He tapped the cigarette on the case then lit it. After inhaling deeply, he blew smoke upward into the frigid night air as he drew his suit coat tightly around him. "What's your name?"

Bai kept watch, just steps away from Chen, at the ready to protect his boss if the situation called for it. Jiang walked up next to Chen's other side. The Kenyan's eyes went from one to the other, his brow beaded with sweat.

"Gacoki."

"Well, Gacoki … I'm Mr. Lin. Chen to my friends, so you may call me Mr. Lin as we are doing business." Chen waited for Gacoki to respond. When he didn't, he continued. "Do you want to know about the last guy who assumed he was getting a shitty deal? Want to know what happened to him?" Gacoki stared at Chen but didn't move or try to speak. "He tried to find another buyer, and he did. They took his loot, gutted him like a fish, then threw him in a river."

Chen walked up to Gacoki. Matched in stature, Chen was able to look dead center into his sunken black eyes. He took the envelope back out of his pocket then pressed it firmly in Gacoki's hand but did not release the envelope. Instead, he placed his other hand on top and pulled Gacoki in close.

"Let me break it down for you," Chen spoke low. "Most people think that there are more guys like you and that you're all disposable. If one of you dies, another one will take your place. You understand?"

Gacoki gave a slight nod.

"Not me, Gacoki. I like to find people I can trust. The more I trust you, the more you'll make. I take care of my people." He let go of the envelope and Gacoki's hands.

Chen didn't give a damn about people, but he did care about money. When he lost one of his good men, he mourned the loss of the income they would no longer bring to him. And it was such a pain to find someone trustworthy and loyal, because when you worked with criminals, everyone had self-interests.

Chen motioned to Bai and Jiang. The two men walked over to the truck and started to transfer the bags into a refrigerated truck used for transporting meat.

Chen continued, "If you're not getting a big enough cut, you could help me with a new cargo. Of course, you really must have balls for this one, but it pays more."

"What is it?" Gacoki put the envelope in his pants pocket.

"Ivory."

Gacoki's features remained rigid, but Chen noticed his eyes had flickered.

"How?"

"Very easy. I need you in Mombasa in January. That's a little over a month from now. Plenty of time to steal a ride on a cargo boat. You get in touch with me when you get there."

Gacoki didn't answer. Chen knew exactly what was going through the man's mind. Ivory meant dealing with the Golden Dragon, which meant more money for him, but it also meant more risk.

Chen added, "The money is triple. It's more dangerous, but I'm sure you can handle it." He held out a black card. Gacoki took it and examined the snakelike gold dragon embossed on the front and the cell number on the back before he slid it into his pocket.

"Call if you want more money." Chen gave a two-finger salute then turned to walk to a black Land Rover. "If I haven't heard from you by the fifteenth, I'll find someone else."

"I'll be there," Gacoki said, then turned back toward the truck.

Chen called out to Bai and Jiang, "You two meet me at the market."

As he turned and walked towards the car, Chen had a good feeling about Gacoki. His eyes were sharp and greedy. He was bringing in the numbers; the family business was booming. His father would have been proud.

Chapter 2: Scene of the Crime

A gray haze wove through tropical trees surrounding the forest by the Ngoka River. Lush green brush lined the meandering, slow-flowing river that divided Cameroon and the Republic of Congo, Africa. Mac's eyes scanned the greenery. She felt the chill of the mid-January morning, not just because the morning temperatures were at a cool sixty-six degrees, but because it was unusually quiet and unsettling.

She shifted uncomfortably under the weight of her heavy armored vest. She believed the vest was unnecessary, but Cameron had insisted.

Movement caught her eye. A dark bobbing head glided away from her through the papyrus grass like a shark searching for prey. It was Abebe, the lead field ranger.

She couldn't see Cameron. He was a former marine, part tech nerd, part action figure, and overall leader of all the rangers. His combat skills and weapon knowledge were invaluable in dangerous situations such as this.

"*Ju-hu-hu-huuh.*" A short bird-like whistle pierced the silence. Mac knew the sound. It was Cameron signaling for Abebe to follow him. The vegetation shook as Abebe darted toward Cameron's direction and disappeared into the trees.

She leaned out the truck's window, quieted her breath, closed her eyes, and listened. It was a trick Abebe had taught her. He had said, 'Sometimes you have to close your eyes to hear better and turn down sound to see better'. He was right. Without the extra confusion of sight, she could better isolate and tune into the sounds of Africa.

She first heard the whisper of the flowing river and quickly disregarded it. Then she focused on a small chorus of *peep*s. They were the sounds of African pygmy geese. Their chatter was quick and irritated as if they were being disturbed.

There you are, she thought. Mac opened her eyes as a sea of iridescent green, brown, and gold colors burst into the air in cyclone of activity. The geese took flight over the treetops, their feathers luminescent in the setting sun.

"*Ju-huuh … ju-huuh.*" Another signal. All was clear.

Cameron slowly emerged from the foliage with his head down. *Not a good sign*, Mac thought as she jumped from the truck then ran in his direction.

"Is he alive?" Mac held her breath, hoping for the best.

Cameron stopped. The look on his face said enough.

"Oh." Mac knew her medical services would not be needed today. "Where is he? It's a male, right? For an elephant to be out here all alone; I'm assuming it must be."

Cameron nodded and waved for her to follow him. He silently led her through the grass and trees to a clearing close to the river's edge. The trees hung over the giant as if to hide the gruesome brutality. Abebe was inspecting the victim. Mac didn't have to get close to know that this wasn't an accident. It was murder.

His face was missing. It had been hacked off from the eyes forward. Thick pink and white flesh shone where his tusks should have been. It was the curve of the rainforest elephant's skull that confirmed it was male. A female would have had a more pronounced angle.

"How long ago?" Mac asked Abebe as he knelt beside the elephant and placed a hand on the giant's back.

"The body is almost cold. They could still be in the area but are most likely not." Abebe swatted absently at a group of flies. Mac found it disturbing the way flies found death so quickly.

"I'm sorry, my friend." Abebe spoke softly as he stroked the elephant's side. The gesture made Mac's heart hurt. Abebe was strong, skilled, and a little chauvinistic, but his actions now showed his compassionate side.

"Look." Cameron pointed to a large patch of flesh that was cut out of the elephant's hide. "This was probably a partial payment to a local for helping them."

"How do you know that?" Mac asked.

"See here?" Cameron traced the wound's edge. "This cut was made by a duller, less sophisticated blade."

Mac leaned forward for a closer look. A huge fly darted at her eyes, startling her. While trying to frantically wave it off, she stumbled, her foot catching on a root, sending her forward with a painful slap on the blood-soaked ground.

She was face to faceless, just inches away from the brutality. Images of the elephant's death flashed in her mind along with the idea he may have still been alive when they butchered his face. Her stomach rolled over in disgust. Feces and the smell of raw meat flooded her nose, as stomach acid rose in her throat.

Mac jumped up and ran to the trees. She stopped, put her hands on her knees, then retched. She followed through with an embarrassing bout of gagging and snot running from her nose. As the newest person on the team, she cursed herself for not being able to keep control. Her face burned, and she could feel her heartbeat in her temples.

She was still bent over, afraid if she stood too quickly her breakfast would make a curtain call, when brown leather boots appeared in her view, as well as a canteen of water. She grasped it with a shaky hand, then took a slow sip.

Cameron's brow furrowed. "That was pretty gross, Red. You okay?"

"I'm sorry," Mac managed to cough out the words as warm tears rolled down her burning face. She gave him an embarrassed smile. "I guess I'm not cut out for this part. I was hoping to give medical assistance to a not-so-faceless elephant."

She stood, wiped her eyes with her hands, then took another sip. The well water, usually not a favorite of hers, tasted cool and refreshing compared to the acid that had made its unwelcome exit from her stomach. To her surprise, neither Cameron nor Abebe were laughing at her rookie mistake.

"No matter how many times I see something like this," Cameron said, "it still sickens me too. I've seen a lot of death in my time, but that doesn't make it easier."

Cameron joined Abebe, and they inspected the scene. Mac decided to keep her distance. She'd already lost enough cool points today. After all, her main job was to care for the injured elephants, particularly the calves, not to investigate poachers. Though lately, she was seeing more dead elephants. But none so recently murdered as this one.

Mac wiped the mud from her hands onto her vest and inspected herself for cuts or anything that would invite unwanted infection, a life-threatening situation this far away from a hospital. Her normally pale skin was pink from months in the sun and muddy from her recent trip to the ground but unmarked. *Good, one less thing to worry about.*

"Do you think it was militia?" Mac asked. "Maybe trading the tusks for weapons or ammunition?"

Abebe answered, "I don't think so. I see five separate tracks … one is barefoot, probably a local tracker. And one is someone we are familiar with."

"Fancy Boots?" Cameron asked.

"Who's Fancy Boots?" Mac pictured an animated cat dressed in a musketeer hat with yellow plumage and over-the-knee boots.

"There have been unique boot prints at some of the slayings," Cameron explained. "Unique enough that they were noted. They're made by Danner M.E.B.'s, which cost about four hundred dollars a pair. Not exactly something you find around here."

"M.E.B.?" Mac asked. "Want to put that in regular-people terms?"

"Marine Expeditionary Boot." Cameron smiled. "For you regular-people."

"Here. I can show you." Abebe waved them over. He pointed to a muddy patch. "See the thick lug design in that boot print." Abebe's finger traced the area.

"That is quite unusual," Mac observed.

"Fancy Boots has possible ties into one of our largest poaching rings," Cameron stated.

"Are you saying this might tie into the Golden Dragon's poaching syndicate?" Mac hoped the answer would be no. The idea that the most wanted poacher kingpin in Africa having his sights on our area was terrifying to her.

Abebe bent down and picked up something.

"What did you find?" Cameron asked.

"A shell casing. They used a Weatherby. Locals can't afford that fire power. I think it's a safe assumption about the Golden Dragon, between this and the boot prints." Abebe put the casing in his pocket.

"That's what I was afraid you'd say." Mac knew it wouldn't be good for their herd, especially Amahle. Amahle was a twelve-year-old female, about to give birth for the first time. A primal urge to protect the elephants rose through her. Love and anger intertwined with an overwhelming helplessness of knowledge that she couldn't protect them all.

"It looks like they may be branching out their territory," Cameron looked at Mac. "This might be a one-off, but it might also be an exploratory kill. Testing the waters on our security—which seems to have failed."

Cameron sniffed and rubbed his face, making it cartoonishly long for a second. He turned and surveyed the area, his eyes squinting at the sunbeams that had managed to fight their way past the thick blanket of branches. "This isn't good. One today means more … and soon."

"What can we do?" Mac's voice came out hoarse and scratchy, sounding weak and more inquisitive than she cared for. *I haven't traveled all the way to Africa to be a maiden in distress.* She cleared her throat, took another sip of water, and spoke in a calmer, more determined tone. "I mean, what are *we* going to do about this?"

"Let's go back to base and I'll launch the drone to see if they're still in the area." Cameron turned, placed a hand on Mac's shoulder, and gave it a little squeeze. "If they come back, we'll be ready. And you need to clean up. You stink."

Chapter 3: A Bird's-Eye View

Three high-definition monitors gave multiple views of the 27,840-acre, or 11266.448-hectares as most metric users would understand, private ranch. It was strategically nestled between Lobéké National Park and the Republic of Congo's Odzala-Kokoua National Park. The ranch was strategically positioned to give wildlife safe passage as they traveled between the protected parks and to block ranchers from purchasing the area to turn it into a big game hunting ranch.

Cameron leaned back in his high-back chair. He pulled his headset down around his neck while he massaged his scalp and scanned the aerial view of lush terrain.

A herd of zebras grazed lazily, all raising their heads in a wave of black and white to the low hum of the drone as it passed by. The grass scenery displayed by the drone's high-definition cameras was soon replaced with a canopy of trees. Dark shapes in the branches caught his eye.

Zooming in to confirm his suspicions, he recognized the western lowland gorilla with the big silver back. "Good morning, *Oupa*." *Oupa*, meaning Grandpa in South Africa, was an old male with twelve unrelated females in his family. Oupa looked up at the drone, only to look away as if bored. He was accustomed to regular invasions of privacy.

Cameron loved his job. He was paid to play with drones, elephants, and to shoot at bad guys. What more could a man want? He watched the video screen as trees flashed by. The drone was an expensive and amazing tool funded by Charles "Chimp" O'Neilson. Chimp earned his nickname by his big ears and a bald head with grey hair sticking wildly out at the sides, giving him an uncanny likeness to the primate.

Cameron thought back to when he first met Chimp, he was assigned to a joint force task team deployed to the U.S. Africa Command to conduct operations for the Department of Defense. Their mission was to delegitimize al-Qaida and their supporters and affiliates who operated in Africa. Cameron was attending a technical conference, demonstrating drones and other sophisticated equipment, when Chimp walked up to his booth. With al-Qaida funding their weapons and supplies by poaching ivory, Chimp was interested in securing his property.

He offered the use of a large portion of his land to help the U.S. Government and Kenyan authorities with their delegitimizing effort in exchange to see how drones would help him in his own anti-poaching efforts. Chimp and Cameron worked together closely for months along with the Kenyan authorities, U.S., and local friendly forces.

In a few months, they were able to destroy the al-Qaida cell's communications, driving the militants away from their stronghold in the outskirts of Lobéké National Park. Their efforts helped the Kenyans recover two tons of illegal ivory, worth two million dollars, before it made its way to the Kenyan port of Mombasa and onto a cargo ship headed for Singapore. In addition, they were also able to save thirty-seven young teenagers from human trafficking.

Chimp was impressed with Cameron's technical expertise and could see the value of using drones for tracking poachers on his ranch. After the mission, Chimp offered Cameron a job. 'My conservation efforts have turned into a war,' Cameron remember Chimp saying. 'My rangers are unprepared, outgunned, and at risk just as much, if not more, than the animals. I could use an expert like you. You'll be in charge, and I can pay you triple what you are earning now.' Cameron didn't reenlist that year.

And now here he was, five years later, leading a team of rangers and still fighting the same bad guys for different reasons. Chimp was due a visit here soon, to check on the drone program and to discuss the more serious issue of a local poaching cell that was getting highly dangerous and more efficient.

His thoughts were interrupted by several muffled *beeps,* a *click,* then the opening of a door.

"Hello, my brother." Abebe stepped in.

"Abebe. How's it going?"

"We were able to acquire twenty more bullets, enough to fill the guns of my men. We'll go to the herd tonight. Keep watch over them."

"Just twenty? What's the problem now? I know we aren't out of money."

"The last case was stolen. It will take weeks to reship." Abebe walked over to Cameron, his eyes darting screen to screen.

"Dammit. Again? This is ridiculous. I'm going to pick up the next crate myself." Cameron exhaled in frustration.

"I suggest we find a different means of ordering."

"You think we have a spy?" Cameron looked up at Abebe.

"I think my men sometimes have mouths to feed and bad decisions take place, but I can't be sure. Either way, I feel it's in our best interest to plan differently. At least to rule them out. They don't understand more stolen guns and more stolen ammo mean more likelihood they'll be shot, and their families will starve."

"They're paid well. I don't think that's the issue." Cameron understood how poor many Africans in the Democratic Republic of the Congo were. The government park field rangers were paid very little, and it was difficult to get supplies. But Chimp paid his rangers enough money to feed their families and to keep them honest.

"The poor are just as fallible as the rich when spending wages. Everyone wants more." Abebe turned to leave.

"Hey, Abebe."

Cameron stood to face him. Cameron made a fist and brought it to his chest. Abebe did the same.

"Brother," Cameron stated.

"Brother," Abebe responded then left.

Mac appeared on one of the screens, sitting and watching the herd. A playful grin crossed Cameron's face as he sat on his chair, took the drone off auto, then started its descent.

Chapter 4: Drone On

The red sun's rays reached out over the African bush, waking the animals in a symphony of chirps, growls, screeches, and whoops. After a morning of death, Mac felt the need to see her family, if anything, to confirm they were all safe. She showered away any indication of the earlier tragedy then quickly headed to her favorite vantage point.

Perched on a large boulder, Mac looked over her knees at the herd of forest elephants that had made the ranch their home. She had driven one of the trucks and parked it as close as she dared without disturbing the herd. The elephants seemed not to mind her as they snorted and trumpeted contentedly, munching on branches, and nuzzling their calves.

Mac was particularly proud of Nala, a three-year-old calf they recently introduced to the herd. Her mother was found dead due to a bullet—a botched poaching event that had shattered a bone in her leg, leading to hours of suffering and eventually her passing.

When Nala first arrived, she was shy and despondent. But all the elephants welcomed the orphan. Her adoptive mother, Shaba, nuzzled and caressed her with her trunk as soon as they met. It didn't take long before she was happy again.

Nala was Mac's last orphaned calf to introduce to the herd ... until the next one arrived. She had been at the ranch for six months and had worked with five orphans already. The orphans varied in ages, but Nala was the youngest they had found, and Mac favored her.

As Mac watched the elephants play, her mind wandered to Keene. Keene was her fiancé, back in Texas. He had died a horrible death.

"I can't believe it's been year since you left," she said out loud.

"What was that, Red?" Cameron's smooth voice asked in her ear.

Mac jumped. She'd forgotten about the earpiece and that this one had a sticky push-to-talk button.

"Hey, sorry," she responded, keeping her voice low as she fiddled with the tactical radio clipped to her belt. "Dang button sticks. How's the air-conditioning? Bet it's rough in there."

"It's a hard life. Your comment earlier … feeling nostalgic?" Cameron asked. Cameron didn't know the details of how Keene died. She hadn't spoken to anyone about him.

"I wouldn't say nostalgic," Mac responded. "I feel like a person having an out-of-body experience. Last year, around this time, I was in Texas, tending small animals like rabbits and cardinals at a sanctuary. Now, I'm in Africa helping to elephants. It's just kinda surreal."

She told a half-truth. It wasn't just being in Africa the last few months—it had been *their* dream to come to Africa together—only, Keene never made it. As images of the dead elephant from the morning flashed through her mind she wondered if this was still *her* dream.

"I know what you mean, Red. This is the stuff you read about, right? Of course, someone must live it to write about it."

Cameron had started calling her Red the day they met. She didn't find it very creative, since her hair was a shocking red, but it was endearing ... in an annoying way.

"Any sign of the poachers?" she asked, changing the subject.

"No. They aren't within range."

A familiar buzzing filled her ears as a quadcopter drone floated down to her right. Though it seemed absurd to her, the prehistoric-looking metal bug made her feel safe, like having a pet or guardian by her side. She had nicknamed the drone Beetlejuice, like the ghost character in that old movie her mother made her watch every Halloween. The drone had a black-and-white design with the ability to cause mischief, reminding her of the unbearable character.

"Hey, Beetlejuice." Mac smiled for the drone's camera. Cameron gave a lighthearted chuckle when she said the name. They all seemed to treat the drone like it was a separate entity and not just a flying camera. People were funny like that.

Ever since Cameron had smiled a "hello" to her, Mac had liked him. Of course, when she first arrived, she was still mourning Keene and had no place or patience for Cameron. Little had she known her inadvertent hard-to-get act had been an attraction and catalyst to building a bond between them. Building to what … a romantic relationship … platonic flirting? She didn't know.

"Sometimes, I think how much easier it was back in Texas." There was no response from Cameron, but she could hear his breathing on the open line.

He finally spoke, "I know this was probably more than you expected. It would be more than anyone would expect."

"This?" Mac chortled. "You mean finding myself in the middle of multiple wars? Conflicts between park rangers, conservationists, poachers, drug lords, and the cruel idiots who don't care about animals' lives?"

"Um, yeah. I think that's succinct."

"Nope," Mac made a popping noise when pronouncing the *p*. "There are just so many things working against us … it's hard to see this ever getting better for these animals."

"There is only one way to eat an elephant."

"What?" Mac exclaimed, confused.

"One bite at a time."

"That is a gross and highly inappropriate analogy, considering all this."

Cameron laughed. "My inappropriate point is any complex issue can be overwhelming, but no matter how challenging, it can be tackled bit by bit, and eventually, it will be gone."

"I get your point. Although, I'm sure there would have been a better way to phrase it."

"I'll work on it." Cameron continued, "You're making a difference, you know. We lost one today, but we've saved a few too."

"You're right." Mac looked again at Nala.

"Of course, I'm right. When am I wrong?" Mac didn't bother to retort, as he added, "Now, head back so I don't worry about you."

The drone climbed back to its viewing height.

"I will," Mac replied, but made no effort to leave.

The morning was starting to heat up. She took a deep breath, taking in the sweet dry grass, earth, and the light sent of citronella from her bug repellant mixing with her salty sweat. She wanted one more minute of watching the herd as they grazed and nuzzled happily. Safe—for the moment.

"Oh, and I forgot to mention," Cameron spoke up again, "we received a tip on the poachers. You and I can take a trip to the market if you feel like it. Do some snooping."

"Hell, yeah! Lead with that next time." She slid quietly off the rock and headed toward the truck.

Chapter 5: Man Cave

Mac arrived at a large wooden structure that resembled a hut. She bounded up the steps to a lobby adorned in wicker furniture and braided straw rugs. Lebron, the youngest worker and her frequent pet sitter, sat at a desk under a ceiling fan made of bamboo. He was finishing up a call on an old-fashioned black phone when she walked in. He was fourteen and usually had an infectious smile, but today, he barely gave a grin.

Behind him, Siyabonga, one of the older rangers was there, speaking quietly in his ear. Mac noticed a gold looking chain around his neck, which would be unusual for someone here to own. Meeting Mac's eyes, Siyabonga stopped talking and quickly stood, his chain disappearing back under his shirt. He straightened his collar before speaking.

"Good morning, Miss Mac."

Siyabonga looked like he was in his twenties, but Mac wasn't sure of his real age. He was easy to spot because of his missing front tooth. She was told he had been at the ranch a long time, almost ten years. He seemed friendly enough and was usually quiet.

"Morning." She focused on Lebron's eyes, raising her eyebrows. "Everything okay?"

Siyabonga answered for them. "Yes, ma'am. I'm helping him with his paperwork."

Mac looked directly at Lebron, waiting for him to answer her.

"Yes, ma'am." Lebron looked shyly down.

Maybe Lebron is embarrassed. Me he had made a mistake, and Siyabonga is disciplining him.

Not wanting to embarrass the boy further, she gave a nod and walked briskly to the back room. She stopped at a secure entry keypad mounted on the wall next to a steel door, then punched in a code. When she heard the accepting *click,* she pushed the heavy door open, and shivered as cool air hit her face.

Cameron sat, looking up at various screens in the control room.

"Roughing it, I see?" Mac chuckled as she walked over to Cameron's chair. He didn't move. She leaned over his shoulder. Fast, rhythmic electric guitars, drums, and the muffled gruff vocals from Metallica's "Enter Sandman" emanated from his headphones.

Her nose was near his short blond hair. She caught the faint hints of chocolate from the black soap he used and of coffee from his morning cup of joe.

"Hey." She tapped his plastic ear covers.

Cameron flinched. A smirk spread across his face as he slid his headphones off his ears then motioned toward the screen. "Just in time to see me land."

On a heavy steel monitor mount were two rows of three monitors, neatly numbered one thru six by bits of white tape with black writing. Screens one through four displayed software that plotted the field ranger movements, bush fires, and other critical information. Screen five displayed Beetlejuice's view, and screen six monitored the drone launchpad.

Beetlejuice had high-tech cameras that could see at night to aid rangers in identifying and potentially stopping poachers. Cameron had modified the drone to also drop paint balls loaded with chili pepper to keep elephants from leaving the parks' boundaries and, on occasion, to surprise a poacher.

On monitor six, Beetlejuice hovered for a moment, then floated gently down to the mini landing pad. Abebe came into the frame. His lean, muscular physique was not lost in the black and white image on the screen, neither was the AK-101 rifle slung over one shoulder. Watching Abebe, Mac sometimes felt like she was more at a military installation than at a private ranch.

"Is Abebe leading the patrol tonight?"

"Yes." Cameron turned his chair to face her. He stood, making no attempt to put distance between them. She had to look up to meet his eyes.

They wore the same brown ranger uniform, except his thick button-up shirt barely fit over his biceps. Cameron's sleeves were rolled up in a traditional military wide fold just above his elbow, exposing his tattoo of an eagle gripping a sword pierced through a heart. The words "Death Before Dishonor" cascaded down the sword in three ribbon banners. Mac remembered asking him about it on the first day. He had told her it was from his days with the Marines and remembered little about the night he got it.

"Are you ready to go sleuthing?" He locked his gaze with hers and raised an eyebrow.

"Sleuthing? Okay, Sherlock, let's get to market and go full-on clue hunting."

"First, we eat," Cameron declared as he stepped closer. "Need to keep your training up."

Mac did her best bodybuilding double-bicep pose.

Cameron whistled, "You've put on some serious muscle, Red. I remember when you got here. A hundred and thirty pounds of average build."

"Thanks a lot."

"I don't mean you didn't look good, Red." Cameron tussled her hair.

"Argh. You know I hate that." She pushed his hand away.

"That's why I do it." He smirked. "I just meant that the muscle makeover was impressive." He pinched one toned bicep as they walked toward the door.

"I guess you want me to thank you for letting me do all the hard labor around here. Moving large bags of food and supplies all in the name of training." Mac took the lead in their quest to the kitchen, as her stomach growled.

"Yeah, and I took you to the market to get your vegan foods and to show you some good protein-rich dishes. Hey, people pay big money for personal trainers back in the States, and you were getting it for free."

"Again, not for free. Hard labor involved."

Chapter 6: Breakfast Not at Tiffany's

The smell of turmeric, coriander, and garlic filled Mac's nose, as she and Cameron walked into the canteen. They sat at one of two large wooden tables.

Cameron took in an exaggerated breath and let it out with an *ah* of approval. "Smells like heaven, Corinne," he called out. A buxom woman in large floral print walked out from the kitchen holding plates of food.

"Of course, love. Puts hair on your chest and meat on your bones." She winked at Mac.

Corinne was what locals referred to as an Afrikaner. She was born in Africa of British descent and spoke with a British accent. Her bright blue eyes stood out against her white hair and skin that never tanned and always looked on the cusp of a sunburn. Everyone was too skinny in Corinne's eyes. And if you weren't too skinny, you were too fat. Mac believed Corinne preferred people who were on the skinny side so that she could feel needed by feeding them.

Abebe walked in, giving a wave. "I'm here just in time. You two haven't eaten all the food yet," he joked, speaking with an accent that sounded like a mix between Cape Kalan English and Corinne's Afrikaans.

Abebe's skin, unlike Corinne's, was deep brown and flawlessly smooth. He had full lips, and a friendly, round face. His eyes were ebony and a subtle dimple in his chin gave him an older look than his twenty-four years.

"I hear you two are going to market." He sat, quickly picking up a spoon.

"I have a lead to follow up on," Cameron replied.

Corinne set two bowls of thick vegetable stew on the table with a plate of bread, then returned to the kitchen and came back with another bowl.

Mac drew one of the bowls to her, then leaned into the aroma saying, "Smells and looks delicious, Corinne."

"Of course. Been cooking it for the last four hours. Enjoy." She disappeared to the back again singing, "Always on My Mind," Willie Nelson style.

"I swear," Cameron stated, "that woman can do more with slow cooking, salt, and pepper, than the top chiefs with all their spices and malarkey."

"Mmmm … I love malarkey." After a few spoonsful, Mac asked, "Who are you riding with tonight, Abebe?"

"Roshan ... Thato ... Bandile ... Siyabonga." Abebe spoke each name between huge spoonsful. "We're keeping a lookout for the poachers in case they return."

"Maybe I can go on a patrol sometime," Mac chimed in looking down at her food. When no one replied, she looked up to notice everyone staring at her. Abebe was in mid-chew. "What?" she stated raising her hands.

"You need to stick to your orphans." Abebe gave Mac a look that reminded her life was different here in Africa and that this was still a vastly male-dominated country.

Mac set her spoon down. "I heard about the all-female unit." They were called the Akashinga or "the Brave Ones and protected the Phundundu Wildlife Park. "I heard they protect the elephants better than the men." Women park rangers were rare, and she hadn't met any personally.

"Don't take it the way it sounded." Cameron gave Abebe the side-eye, which he quickly shrugged off. "You don't want to be out there, Mac. The poachers don't care about the animals, the rangers, or that you're a volunteer. They will kill you."

"I want to help. I don't want to shoot anyone, just offer another set of eyes, or be there if an elephant is injured." Mac had wanted to make a statement more than an argument.

"You're helping more here than by putting your life on the line —let Abebe do that." Cameron nonchalantly pointed his spoon at Abebe.

Roshan, Abebe's second-in-command, walked in. Roshan's skin was very dark, his short hair accentuated a high forehead and small ears. A thin mustache adorned his lip like someone had drawn it on with a pencil.

"We are ready to go," Roshan addressed Abebe and gave Cameron and Mac a nod.

"Thanks, my friend." Abebe put down his spoon. "I leave you both here. Good luck." After Abebe turned to leave, Roshan quickly grabbed a handful of bread, giving Mac a wink before he ran to catch up with Abebe.

Mac knew what they said was true. She didn't want to run into any poacher. But she had a feeling that the longer she stayed in Africa, the bigger a possibility it was, and she would prefer to be prepared.

"Anyway, the market?" Mac picked the conversation back up.

Cameron stood. "I have to get something before we leave." He turned back to Mac. "I'll pick you up shortly. We'll take the Jeep on this trip."

"What are you getting?"

"My Glock," Cameron stated matter-of-factly.

Mac raised her eyebrows. "Do you think the market is that unsafe?"

"Better to have it and not need it." Cameron paused for a second before saying, "Hey, aren't you from Texas? Didn't they issue you a gun when you were born?"

"Ha ... ha. Let's just hope we don't have to use your gun."

Chapter 7: This Little Pig Went to Market

Dirt ruts, divided by a strip of thick green grass, were as close as one could call a road on the ranch. Mac held on as Cameron steered the Jeep over rough terrain, through mud, and across streams of water as high as the tops of the tires. She worried about the Jeep stalling in the water and having to free it—who knew what lurked in its depths?

Mac took in the immenseness of Africa and how long it would take them to get to a market.

"I never thought I would miss Walmart," she yelled over the engine noise. "I definitely *did not* appreciate it as much as I do now. Seemed a lot more convenient to go to the store in Texas."

She envisioned life back home, sitting at a local bookstore drinking coffee and hanging out with her mom for dinner. A pang of sadness traveled through her at the image.

"Missing home, fries, and apple pie?" Cameron asked.

"How did you know?"

"You had that longing look."

"Do you ever miss home?"

"Me? Nah, I don't have anyone in the States anymore. My parents passed away a long time ago. Dad had cancer and Mom just passed away too soon. I stayed with my grandmother through my senior year of high school, then she passed not long after I joined the Marines. Longevity doesn't run in the family. I guess that's why I don't really fear death. Everyday above ground is beating the odds for me."

"That's the first time I've heard you mention your family." Mac had no idea his parents had died and wondered why the subject of family had never come up.

"I'm a live-in-the-now kind of person. I only visit the past every once in a great while." He smiled at her, and she couldn't help but smile back, even though she felt a little sorry for him.

Mac sat back and watched the trees. Sometimes, she caught glimpses of the apes that lived here, however today the only things in the branches were leaves.

"Almost out." Cameron pointed ahead to where the rutted road turned onto a solid dirt road that would soon put them at the ranch gates.

"Which market are we going to?" Mac asked.

"Lobila. We're going to talk to Mamadou. I have word that he has information that may help us."

"Information about the people that killed the elephant we found?" she asked.

"Information about poaching, yes. But I don't know the details."

"What are they for?" She pointed behind her at two milk crate sized boxes and a bag.

"Food and medical supplies. Word is a local was badly hurt. I think he may be one of our poachers."

"Are the medical supplies for thanks or for a bribe?"

"Both. Money's no good if there's no food to buy. At least I know it will help someone."

Cameron drove up to the ranch's gate; a railroad-like crossing arm and a small shack. Two armed men slowly emerged from the hutch, gave a nod to them, and pushed down on the short end of the crossing arm to raise it vertical. Cameron gave them a tip of his boonie hat and drove through. Mac glanced back at the men and the modest wood sign that declared the ranch was private property and that "Poachers Will Be Shot". She wondered if that actually worked.

About an hour later, a familiar collection of broken-down wooden sheds and torn umbrellas came into view. This was probably the third time she had been to this small village market, but she was still surprised at the level of poverty.

A horde of children, most of them barefoot, ran up to the Jeep, smiling and reaching for them. They knew the Americans brought treats. Cameron parked, then grabbed one of the bags. He jumped down into the sea of children, and Mac did the same.

Small fingers touched her skin as she moved through the crowd. They followed her like ducklings. They did this every time she came to the market. The children chattered at her, but Mac still struggled with the language and could only make out a few words.

A group of girls giggled with their hands over their mouths. Young boys looked in her direction and snickered shyly. She kept hearing the words *rooikop akkedis*. Cameron let out a quick snort of laughter.

"What are they saying?" Mac asked.

"They've given you a new nickname." He pointed to one of the boys. "Do you speak English?"

"Yes," the boy said, then smiled proudly.

"Tell the lady what you said." Cameron grinned as if to show the boy he wasn't in any trouble.

"You remind me of the red-headed rock lizard," he stated and giggled.

"Oh, really?" She turned to the boy and gave him a wink. The children laughed, and the girls came to touch her bright red hair.

"Alright, alright." Cameron reached into his pockets and brought out a handful of hard candies. The children swarmed him like pigeons in a New York City park when a handful of birdseed was thrown.

In seconds the candy was gone.

"Okay, okay. *Goed okay, alles weg.*" Cameron spoke in Afrikaans while showing empty hands. The children squealed with laughter, then ran with their treasure.

"How much candy do you have stashed?"

"Oh, the last time I was in the States, I brought back a five-pound bag. I'm halfway through it. I love these kids. Even with a hard life, they still manage a smile for a small bit of sugar."

Mac noticed the older children in the market. Their smiles had faded, now that they were old enough to work. One boy, about thirteen, carried a platter of peppers. Another carried a large jug on his head. Many more teens were scattered throughout the market. All wore clothes that looked either too small, too big, or too old and ragged. The clothing ranged from traditional threaded shirts, full of bright oranges, browns, and whites, to old T-shirts and shorts.

"Look, there he is." Mac motioned with her head to the familiar wooden structure sandwiched between two white umbrellas. On one side, a woman in long braids and a brightly flowered skirt sold a handful of tomatoes, a bunch of long green onions, and some unrecognizable root, all spread out on a small table. On the opposite side, under a white umbrella, a thin bald man sat asleep in a plastic chair. His chin lay against his chest, placing his neck at awkward angle. He had a three-legged table with knockoff British soccer jerseys and six shoes, all mismatched.

The booth in between the umbrellas was slightly nicer with a display of several traditional drums and small handmade bags that looked to be made of crocodile. Wearing a crisp white Kufi hat and a large baggy cream shirt, Mamadou looked wealthier than most of the vendors. He tended to know a lot and would talk for a price, which allowed him such luxuries.

Cameron's eyes darted around, as if skimming the crowd to see if anyone was watching.

"Follow me, and don't say anything," Cameron told her. Mac started to protest, but then he spoke to her softly, "Look, I'm not trying to be mean or sexist. It's just still a very male-dominated society and Mamadou is—"

"Traditional," Mac replied flatly. "Maybe I should wait here then." Mac was annoyed at the idea of being seen as less of a person.

"No, I need us to look together. It's less obvious, Red. I promise, you can boss me around later if it makes you feel better." He smiled as he put his hand on her shoulder.

"Okay, deal. I will boss you around later." She planned on keeping that deal.

The two of them walked toward Mamadou. Cameron grabbed her hand as if they were a couple. Mac felt awkward since they had never held hands. *This feels kind of nice. It's been a long time since I held someone's hand.*

On the way, they stopped at several tables and even bought some tomatoes and onions from the woman with long braids. Mac chatted with the woman about her children for a few minutes before Cameron gently pulled her in the direction of Mamadou's booth. He stopped and examined one of the drums intently.

"Do you see what you are looking for?" Mamadou asked.

Mac looked around Cameron at the sleeping man. He hadn't moved. Given the situation, she suppressed the urge to see if he was still breathing.

"Not yet." Cameron replied, outlining a pattern on the drum with his finger. "Heard you may have some information on a recent hunting trip."

Mamadou grabbed a purse that hung from a hook and showed it to Cameron. "I have a beautiful purse for your lady." He tilted his head toward Mac. She blushed, not knowing whether to be insulted the man addressed Cameron and not her, or to be happy at the idea they were a couple.

"Specifically," Cameron continued, "about the poaching of an elephant in Odzala."

"What would you give for this purse? It is made of real crocodile."

"Isn't that illegal?" Mac chimed in. Cameron gave her a cautionary look.

"This one died of old age," Mamadou answered Mac by addressing Cameron, which infuriated her. Cameron gave her hand a gentle squeeze she assumed was to comfort and to remind her to ignore the man.

Mac glanced again at the sleeping man. He still hadn't moved. She looked more closely and was relieved to see the slow rise and fall of his chest.

"He is not dead," Mamadou stated flatly. "Just had too much of his uncle's *lotoko*. Horrible stuff."

Mac looked at Cameron questionably.

"Moonshine," Cameron responded. He then took the bag from around his shoulder and opened it, just a bit, so Mamadou could see the medical supplies. "I have food as well. More in my Jeep. I hear you have a family and someone that may need help. Someone who is sick, maybe very sick."

Mamadou's smile never faltered. "What do you want to know?"

"I want to talk to the local man who took the poachers onto private property."

"We are a poor community. Many men act as guides to feed their families."

"I'm not interested in why and I'm not the authorities. I'm looking for the men who hired him."

Mac noted the contemplation in Mamadou's eyes. Cameron leaned in close. "Loyalty will get him nothing but hungry children without a father. I can help. I just want information. You know I keep my word, my friend. Have I not taken care of you and your family?"

Mamadou seemed to ponder Cameron's words. "He is very sick. He has a wound that has been infected. I can arrange a meeting if you bring a doctor. No authorities. He has a fever and needs western medicine."

"I can do that," Cameron replied.

"No arrests." Mamadou looked intently at Cameron's eyes.

"No arrests."

"You give me supplies now?"

"I will give you some of the food now and then more supplies when the doctor and I see him."

It was Mamadou's turn to check if either the sleeping man or the woman were listening. Mac noticed a milky veil on Mamadou's eyes, dulling the usual brightness seen in younger eyes. Cataracts were one of the many signs of poor health care in the Congo.

Mamadou leaned close to Cameron, whispered in his ear, then stood straight, as if a decision had been made. Cameron handed him the bag he had slung over his arm, then Mamadou handed him one of the drums.

"*Dankie*," Mamadou said. "Enjoy and please come again."

Cameron turned and started back toward the Jeep, handing the drum to one of the children. Mac almost had to jog to keep up with his long strides.

"What's the rush?"

"We need to pick up some things."

They got to the Jeep. Once they were inside and away from prying eyes and ears, Mac asked, "Are we coming back?"

"Yes ... I wish I had time to drop you off at the park. I shouldn't have brought you."

"Do you think it's going to be dangerous?"

"I don't know." Cameron started the Jeep, then drove until he reached National Road 10, then headed south.

"Where are you going to find a doctor?"

"I have friends nearby in Moloundou, a Doctors Without Borders kind of setup. I hope they're still in the area."

Mac wondered how exactly the rest of this day was going to go.

"What are you thinking about, Red? Are you worried? If you really want me to take you back—"

"No, I was just thinking that more people would understand and appreciate what they have in the States if they visited other countries."

"From your lips to God's ears. There are a lot of people who don't want to know. I mean, once you know, you might have to make a conscious decision about whether you're going to care and do something about it or if you're going to just focus on your own life."

"On one hand," Mac replied, "I don't understand why people wouldn't do something. But on the other, there are so many problems in the world … which one do you choose? And if you do choose to care, there's so much corruption, that answer could be wrong too. Hurts my head."

"My head would hurt, too, if I looked at it that way. I pick a point and head toward it. My job is to help the animals on the ranch. It's someone else's job to help with poverty, public health, and clean air. I care about those things too. Just nothing I can do about them."

Mac sighed. "I wish I could turn my brain off."

Cameron patted Mac's knee. His touch, though brief, sent a small electric charge through her. She wondered if he was flirting or being friendly. Mac pulled a blanket from the back, rolled it into a ball, then stuffed it between her head and the steel frame of the Jeep. Closing her eyes, she tried to *not* think what it would be like to feel his lips on hers.

Chapter 8: Chimp

Charles "Chimp" O'Neilson was catching a catnap in his lavish eight-bedroom estate house. His twenty-eight-acre property was nestled in the Congo not far from his ranch. It was surrounded by lush greenery and absolute privacy. His family had owned the property for half a century. He inherited it when his parents died, as well as the family's fortune that helped fund his conservation efforts.

A harsh *ring* interrupted his sleep. He mumbled to himself as he left the comfort of his cushioned chair. The scraping of his slippers on the tile floor seemed to echo in the empty house. Chimp had never married and had no heir. He had dedicated his life to preserving the wildlife of Africa. Though he never regretted his efforts, he often reflected on the women he could have pursued, the family he could have had, and the time he let slip by.

He picked up the large black handset of the rotary dial phone. Like him, the phone was a relic from the '60s. He'd bought it because he liked the weight and the comfort of the handset. He hated the flatness of cell phones and the way people were obsessed with looking at them every few minutes.

"Yes?" he answered.

"Charles, hello old friend," a familiar British accented voice greeted him. He knew who it was immediately. Kendalie was the only person he let call him Charles.

"Kendalie! How are you? How's the family?"

"We are all well, thank you." There was a slight pause.

"What is it, old friend?" Chimp hoped it was good news, for once.

"Another shipment of guns has been stolen. I don't think it's someone here tipping the shipment info, as we first suspected."

So much for good news, he supposed. Chimp knew the "someone" he was referring to the local authorities. "Who do you think it is then?"

"I think it is an inside job."

"Are you inferring it's someone at my ranch?" Chimp sat, leaning back into his study chair, running his rheumatic fingers through his grey hair.

"I was able to track the guns through my channels. I lose them when after they hit transportation."

"Well, that is disappointing."

"I may also have leads on a big shipment of ivory. My sources have told me the Dragon is making a move to ship a large stock of inventory. I will know more by tomorrow. Can you get to Mombasa in the next couple of days?"

"I cannot my friend. However, I can send someone … Cameron."

"I hope so. This may be one of the largest shipments we've seen." Kendalie's tone was somber. "I just wish we could have stopped them earlier."

Chimp considered this. Throughout the years he and Kendalie had been a part of many ivory raids.

Thousands of elephant tusks were confiscated, which also meant thousands of elephants had died.

"Why do you need to tell me in person?"

Kendalie chuckled, "You know me too well, my friend. I did not call just about the guns … I need a favor." He paused, as if he felt guilty to ask for assistance. "I need help with a farming village that is having troubles with elephants raiding their crops. I am working with a local charity to provide bee hives to deter the elephants. I just need two more weeks and someone to visit in person to calm and reassure them. I cannot go there myself and you are the only one I know that can work with the locals. But I know you are … not feeling well."

"Unfortunately, you are correct. I tire easily. Although I do have a volunteer here who is very good with the elephants and people. A caretaker from the states. She can assist Cameron."

"Great! Thank you, my friend." Kendalie let out a long exhale. "You know the place and time."

"Yes, of course, at —"

"I am not on a clear line," Kendalie broke in.

"Ah, then I know the place." Chimp and Kendalie always met at Fort Jesus when in Mombasa, by noon.

"Thank you again and be careful my friend."

"You worry too much, but I will." Chimp knew Kendalie worried just enough. Many conservationists were being murdered for their crusades against poaching … Dian Fossey, Wayne Lotter, and Ranger Anton Mzimba, just to name a few.

Chimp hung up. He wished he could meet Kendalie in person, but he had other more pressing matters, and his health was working against him. The journey to the ranch would be hard enough. He had planned to visit the ranch next Saturday to speak with Cameron. In light of Kendalie's request, he would need to bump it up to tomorrow.

Time was getting short for Chimp, plus it was getting harder to know who to trust. *I need to tie up some business before it's too late.* He looked around his home. *It is a shame I never had children to pass the torch to. I would have liked to hear the laughter and watched them grow and play.* He let out a long sad sigh. *Too late now.*

Chimp was not young, and death was inevitable. Without any family, he had to ensure his ranch and home property would not fall under greedy hands and turned into hunting grounds. Cameron was the only person he knew who could handle the task.

Chapter 9: An Apple a Day

The Jeep bounced hard as Cameron turned off the smooth dirt road onto a smaller dry and rutted ground path, waking Mac up. She stretched and cracked her neck, delighting in the machine gun popping by the gas bubbles bursting, followed by a relief of pressure.

"Where are we going to find a doctor?" Mac asked yawning.

"Not exactly a doctor, a nurse practitioner. There's a village, not far from here, where a U.S. funded health organization is inoculating children. I have an old friend there."

"Your friend will help out a criminal?" Mac looked at Cameron, whose eyes stayed focused on the path as he weaved the Jeep around the larger rocks.

"Medical professionals care about healing people, not about judging them. Well, first they fix them, then they judge them silently to themselves." He snickered at his own joke. "Plus, they understand it's not all black-and-white out here. There's a lot of gray area and different cultures."

Before Mac could ask what he meant, two white tents with a big red cross on the side of each came into view. "I take it we're here."

Many women, children, and people who Mac guessed were medical staff because of their white smocks, walked around the small camp. An attractive man with a thick beard and dad bod seemed to recognize Cameron then walked swiftly toward them.

"There's Michael," Cameron said as he parked the Jeep. Cameron jumped out and Mac followed.

"Cameron! Long time no see. How have you been?" Michael gave Cameron a big hug.

"I've been good. Michael, this is Red. She works with me at the ranch."

"I'm Mac. He's not creative with nicknames."

Michael laughed and offered his hand as he led them to one of the bigger tents, "Nice to meet you." They shook hands as they walked at a quick clip. His grip was firm, but gentle. "So, to what do I owe this honor? Rachelle will be very happy to see you."

Cameron seemed to blush at Michael's statement. "Um, we're actually here on business."

"Oh?" Michael's brow furrowed. "Hopefully, everyone is alright at the ranch."

"Yes, but there *is* someone who needs your assistance."

Michael flipped open the tent's mesh flap, and they went inside. Five cots were lined side by side, each one occupied with a child. Some children were crying and being soothed by their mothers, while other children were looking wide-eyed at the people attending them. All were so thin that Mac wondered how the medical workers found needles small enough for such fragile arms.

In the far corner, a beautiful blond woman looked up from the thin arm she was cleaning with alcohol. A big smile spread across her face and her eyes seemed to light up when she saw Cameron.

"I'll be right with you." She waved excitedly.

Mac turned to see Cameron give the woman a nod and a coy smile back. "So that's —"

"Rachelle. I knew her in the military. We worked together."

Judging from the glances and smiles between them, Mac assumed they were more than coworkers. The lyrics to "Hey Jealousy" by the Gin Blossoms suddenly came to mind. Rachelle looked a lot like Kate Hudson, and Mac wished she didn't.

"Here." Michael pointed to some chairs. "Have a seat. I'm sure you're thirsty, and I have a special stash for special guests. Be right back."

As Michael ran off, Mac and Cameron watched as Rachelle spoke soothingly to a preteen boy. "Now, be brave and I will give you a sweet."

The boy looked at Rachelle, then nodded slowly and sat up straight, keeping his eyes locked on hers. Rachelle pinched what skin she could get from his bony arm and smoothly pierced it with the needle. Just as the boy turned to look at his arm, she had a band aid on it and was handing him a lollipop.

"You did well, buddy. Now stay here with your sister for a bit." She looked at the girl, probably two years older than the boy. "Stay for twenty minutes." Rachelle took another lollipop out of her pocket and handed it to the sister, who beamed accenting pronounced dimples in her cheeks. "Wait until someone in a white shirt tells you to go. We also have some food for you to take home. Okay?" The girl nodded, then suddenly embraced Rachelle in a hug. Rachelle looked to be taken off guard—only for a second—before she wrapped her arms around the child.

"Thank you. Now you take care of yourself and your brother."

Rachelle headed toward Mac and Cameron. Cameron stood and held out his arms as Rachelle came in for hug.

"What are you doing here?" Rachelle asked. "I'm so happy to see you." She lingered in their embrace.

Rachelle and Cameron looked at each other for a moment before Rachelle's eyes begrudgingly left Cameron's face and focused on Mac. They slowly broke away from the hug.

"Hi." Mac held up her open hand in a quick wave. "I'm Mac."

"Oops ... sorry," Cameron said. "Missed the introduction." Seeing Rachelle again seemed to affect Cameron's composure as he struggled for words. "Red, I call her Red, works with me at the ranch. She helps with the orphans."

"Pachyderm orphans," Mac clarified.

"That must be exciting work," Rachelle said.

"It definitely isn't dull."

Michael returned with two cans.

"Shut the front door," Mac exclaimed. "Is that Cherry Coke?" Her mouth watered.

"Been saving these for a special occasion. It's not often we get company." Michael held out the cans. "Now they aren't the coldest, but they aren't warm either."

Mac bent the tab to open the can as soon as she took it from Michael. After hearing the fizz of carbon dioxide, she touched the cool can to her lips. Small, carbonated bubbles tickled her nose as she took a sip. The sweet cherry-flavored syrup and refreshing liquid were heavenly. It had been months since her last soda.

As she slowly enjoyed every sweet liquidly moment, Cameron drank his Cherry Coke in what seemed to be three big gulps, followed by a tent-shaking belch. The tent erupted in children laughing and giggling. *It's good to hear them laugh,* Mac thought.

"Still a pig," Rachelle said and hit him in the arm.

"Better out than in," Michael and Cameron proclaimed in unison, resulting in more laughter.

Mac felt good laughing and being with people who shared her own culture. "Michael, you're my new best friend," she declared.

Michael's face erupted into a charming smile.

"Michael can get anything. He's like Radar in the sitcom *M*A*S*H*," Rachelle said.

"Who?" Mac asked.

Cameron and Rachelle groaned.

"Don't worry," Michael responded. "I had to catch a few shows before I knew what the heck they were talking about. I think it's a military-old-people thing."

"Thanks," Rachelle stated blandly. "So, do you need my help with something?"

"Why do you assume I came here to ask for something?"

Rachelle raised her left eyebrow and pursed her lips.

"Okay. You got me." Looking around the tent, Cameron asked, "Do you have somewhere a little more private where we can talk?"

"We can speak in the med truck," Rachelle told them, then turned to Michael. "Bed two has ten more minutes, and bed three is waiting for treatment. Then we can call it a day."

"On it." Michael dutifully went to bed three.

Rachelle led the way out of the tent to a white medical truck. She opened the back door, and they climbed in among the clutter of supplies.

"So, what's this about?" Rachelle asked.

"I need you to come with me to check on a man who has been injured. Maybe shot. I don't know how bad he is."

"My God, why didn't you just bring him?"

"Because it's more complicated than that."

"Go on." Rachelle sat on a box, then leaned back with her fingers steepled under her chin, like a psychiatrist waiting for a patient to talk about how much their mother screwed up their life.

"He's probably a poacher, and the only way I'm going to get any information out of him is if I bring a doctor and medical supplies."

"And here I figured you missed me."

Again, Mac noticed a look between them, a deep familiarity.

"Will you come?" Cameron asked.

A small part of Mac hoped she couldn't.

Rachelle gave a heavy sigh, "When do we go and what do you need?"

"I knew I could depend on you." Cameron gave her a quick peck on the cheek and then started out the truck's door. "Thirty minutes and bring anything you can for a guy with wound that probably is infected by now." Cameron hopped out. "I'll be back in a minute. Coke's gone through me already. Where's the latrine?"

"Just head to the back of the camp. You'll see the setup."

Cameron started to jog off, and Rachelle leaned out the back of the truck. "I'll need Michael's help. Stop by the tent and let him know."

He waved his hand and didn't look back as he called to her, "The more the merrier."

Rachelle settled back into the truck, grabbed an olive-green bag, then preceded to open and close metal drawers, grabbing supplies as she went. The clinking and scraping of the metal made Mac's teeth hurt.

"Just curious." Mac sat on the back edge of the truck with her arms crossed, watching Rachelle ransack the supplies. "I noticed it didn't bother you that the patient is a poacher. You aren't worried?"

"Michael and I were up north treating people with Ebola last year. I'm more afraid of that than an injured poacher."

"Fair enough," Mac replied. "So how do you know Cameron? I mean, I know the military, but how'd you meet?"

"We worked in the same unit during a TDY—a temporary duty—at Al Dhafra Air Base near Abu Dhabi in the United Arab Emirates. We also dated a little."

Well, she threw out that personal detail as if it were trivial ... or maybe she's trying to see my reaction.

Rachelle continued without further prompting. Speaking fast and factual. "It was a little serious, then I got a promotion and Cameron wanted to leave the service and go to Africa—felt he would be of better use there ... well, here. Personally, I think he got fed up with government bullshit. Anyway, we went our separate ways."

"But you're here now."

Rachelle paused her packing for a second, then continued, "I got out of the service about a year ago. I go where the children are. I wish I could do more for them here ... have a better setup ... maybe someday." She shrugged, then continued to raid the supplies.

Conflicting feelings flooded Mac's mind, feelings about Keene and feelings she hadn't explored about Cameron. Knowing Cameron dated this smart beautiful woman, intimidated her. To her relief, Michael walked up.

"Cameron said we are going on a little field trip," Michael's voice was chipper; he had a warm, contagious attitude about him.

"Yes," Rachelle answered. "I'm just getting some supplies. I don't know how injured this man is, so I'll prepare for the worst." She tossed Michael the bag.

It *clanked* when he caught it. "Our little patient good? Did you send him and his sister home with some food?"

"Yes, all happy. I sent them home with some porridge." Michael took the bag in one hand and held out his hand to help Rachelle out of the truck. They all headed toward the parked Jeep.

"Come on." Cameron was leaning against the vehicle, looking at his watch. "It's getting late."

"You always were a stickler about time," Rachelle smirked as they all piled in.

"And you were always late."

"Are you two going to be like this the entire time?" Michael groaned.

"I'll behave if he does," Rachelle teased.

"And you know I can't promise to behave." Cameron put the Jeep in reverse.

Mac snickered at the banter but wished she had passed on the invitation that morning to join Cameron on this trip. She was uncomfortable about dealing with both a poacher and a beautiful ex-girlfriend. The poacher, she could handle.

Chapter 10: I Like My Eggs Poached

The Jeep pulled into a small rural village where mud brick houses with pointy thatched roofs lined the road. Cameron slowed the Jeep. Some of the houses were covered in what looked like graffiti. Mac recognized the village; it wasn't far from the ranch.

"With the distance and the timing of this man's injuries, it is possible he was involved." Mac turned to face Rachelle and Michael. "It wouldn't have been far to go from his village to the location of the elephant; even on foot."

"In your experience," Mac looked at Rachelle and Michael, "why do you think people here poach?"

Michael replied, "Most of the villages are made up of farming families." He leaned forward, resting his head against the side of Mac's seat. "There are usually four or five children per family, and they're put to work young. Some of the children are given up for adoption because their parents can't feed them. If you had to choose between an animal and your child, what would you choose?"

Rachelle added, "Poverty can make people desperate. Can you imagine giving up one of your kids so that the others don't starve?"

"That's one story," Mac alleged.

"What do you mean?" asked Michael.

"I heard some want flashy cars, women, and booze. Just like a lot of people want. Problem is, they aren't used to the money or have the education to know what to do with it. They spend it quickly, then go back for more." Mac frowned, "I compare it to the drug pushers in a bad neighborhood. Guess we'll see which one this guy is."

"Look. We are not here to judge this guy," Cameron said. "He's a small fish in a giant pond. I'm after the people above him." He stopped the Jeep. "Okay, there it is." Cameron pointed to a hut set furthest away from the road. "When we get in there, let me do all the talking. You guys"—Cameron's eyes focused on the rearview mirror and the occupants in the back— "just take care of the medical problem." He looked at Mac. "I want you to wait here."

"What? No!" Mac looked at Cameron, then the others, waiting for one of them to come to her defense. They didn't.

"I need you to watch the hut. If you see anyone, honk." He sighed., "I'm not leaving you out, if that's what you're thinking. We may need a quick escape." He reached in front of Mac, opened the glove compartment. "This is a 9mm Glock 19." He took a gun out and handed it to her. "Keep it in your lap. You know how to use it."

"Don't you need it?" She took it, checked the safety, then put it back in the glove compartment.

"Best to not go in armed; he may not talk." Cameron leaned backward looking at Rachelle and Michal. "You guys ready?"

"Yep." Michael gave a small salute.

"Ready when you are," Rachelle replied.

The three stepped out of the Jeep. Cameron and Michael grabbed the medical supplies. Before they could get to the door, Mamadou opened it and waved for them to quickly come in.

Mac looked at the open glove compartment. *This is ridiculous. Why would anyone care if we're helping someone.*

She closed the glove compartment, then climbed over the gear box into the driver's seat. The windows were down, but she couldn't hear voices from the small mud house. In fact, everything was oddly quiet and dark. As she looked around, she was sure the village was abandoned.

"This is boring," she snorted to herself. The sun had set, so Mac tried to pick out planets and constellations in darkening sky to pass the time. She had spotted Jupiter and was looking for Orion when a loud *crack* came from nearby bushes.

Mac sunk low in the seat. A murmur of male voices and the crunching of grass came from the direction of the noise. Someone was out there.

Chapter 11: The Interrogation

The stench of putrefaction filled Cameron's nose. He held back an instinctive gag, as the Coke he drank earlier made an acidic reappearance in the back of his throat. Rachelle and Michael seem to be unaffected. *Another day in paradise for them*, he supposed.

Rachelle knelt beside the ill man. "What's his name?" she asked without looking at Mamadou.

Mamadou ignored the request for his name.

"Okay. How about, when was he brought here?" Mamadou still did not answer.

"Hey, there? Can you hear me?" Rachelle asked the injured man, snapping her fingers in front of his face. "Do you speak English?"

"He can understand you," Mamadou answered.

"Ah, he speaks!" Rachelle's curt words displayed her growing irritation.

Michael joined Rachelle and started to inspect a bloody rag on the man's leg. Cameron decided to stay where he was in the doorway, out of the injured man's view.

"Looks like NF." Michael handed Rachelle a scalpel.

Rachelle made a small incision in what looked like purple skin. She slid a gloved finger in the wound. Cameron wrinkled his nose in disgust.

"The affected tissue is starting to feel soft," Rachelle remarked. "It hasn't yet separated along the fascial plane." She looked at Cameron. "NF is necrotizing fasciitis, or flesh-eating bacteria, if you want a more graphic name. Good thing we got here." She held her hand out toward Michael. "Hand me the IV." He handed her a needle as he prepared a tube, a bag of antibiotics, and an expandable IV stand.

Mamadou carried a box of supplies to the corner and started to inspect the contents. Cameron walked over to him as he did so.

"Has he said anything about what happened to him?" he asked.

"Yes," Mamadou mumbled without looking up. "He said they were sent to get the tusks of an elephant. He was promised he would be able to keep some of the meat for his family and would get money. They spent several days traveling into the jungle. When they found nothing, he was told to lead them into the outer edges of a ranch."

"Which one?" Cameron asked.

"I do not know specifics. I assume yours. It is the closest to our village." He continued to rifle through the food, pocketing the spam and beans. "They found tracks to a lone elephant. Followed it to a river. That is where they killed it."

Bingo, Cameron thought. *This is our lead.*

"What happened to him?" Cameron pointed to the man who was groaning as Rachelle and Michael cleaned his wound. Sweat dripped from the man's brow, his face frozen in a painful grimace.

"That was all I could get from him at the time. His fever came quickly, and he goes in and out of consciousness. You may have better luck. He should be awake now from the pain."

Cameron approached the man as his friends worked.

"I can drain it and stitch it," Rachelle stated flatly. "It won't be pretty, but he should live given all the antibiotics I'm about to push. The infection should clear up."

"I have been draining it," Mamadou spoke up.

Rachelle looked at Mamadou. "You did well. Probably saved his life." He nodded his thanks for her compliment.

"We came just in time with the antibiotics," Michael said to Cameron. "Another day or two, and the infection would have spread."

This fact didn't faze Cameron. He was there for information, not sympathy. He wasn't going to bring him to the authorities, but he felt the man got everything he deserved. He didn't carry the same views as Michael and Rachael.

He loudly asked the patient, "Can you tell me what happened to you? Who were the men that hurt you?"

"He is not deaf," Mamadou stated, head down, still sifting through the supplies.

"What is your name? Who hired you?" Cameron repeated slightly softer.

"Can you give him a minute?" Rachelle looked annoyed. "He's in a lot of pain. Give the drugs time to work."

"I can't risk him passing out, and if we leave, he'll probably bolt." Cameron glanced at Mamadou who shrugged.

"Try this." Cameron handed a juice box from his pocket to Michael.

"You just carry around juice?" Michael poked the straw into the box and held it to the man's dry lips. He didn't hesitate to drink. The man's eyes lit up as he tasted the juice.

"I also have candy," Cameron added. "Always be prepared, that's the boy scout's motto."

"You were a boy scout, Cameron?" Rachelle asked with genuine sounding interest.

"No, but I did watch the Scouts Guide to the Zombie Apocalypse."

Michael chuckled.

The man on the makeshift cot stared at Cameron with cloudy brown eyes. After letting out a long breath, the man spoke in a language Cameron didn't understand.

"What is he saying? I'm not as familiar with that dialect." Cameron looked at Mamadou, but it was Michael who answered.

"It's Kituba, a mix between French and Dutch."

"So, you can understand him?"

"We both can," Rachelle replied not looking up, tending to her patient. "Michael's better at speaking the language, though."

"Okay, Michael, ask him his name and who he was with." Cameron watched the man but listened to Michael.

"*Ngeye Niwmbuaku nami*? What is your name?" Michael spoke in Kituba, then repeated it in English. "We are friends. We are here to help."

"*Mono I Mansueki*," the man replied and weakly lifted his head from the pillow.

"He says his name is Mansueki."

"Ask him what happened to him."

Michael spoke to Mansueki, who gave a long reply, then Michael turned to Cameron. "He said they traveled to find an elephant. They made him go onto the ranch because he was able to pick up the trail of a single male. There were five of them. One of them an American. He had given them guns and special glasses to see in the dark." Michael paused as he listened to Mansueki.

"Interesting," Cameron said as Michael focused on Mansueki's words.

"After they killed the elephant, they headed back to the village. They had given him meat and money. When they reached the main path, two of the men decided they were hungry and wanted to cook the meat he had earned for his family. When he refused, and they knocked him down. That's when the stick went into his leg."

"Then what?" Cameron asked. Michael relayed the question, and Mansueki answered.

"The big American told the men to stop and to carry the tusks somewhere. He wrapped his leg and brought him to the edge of the village. He walked the rest of the way home. Then he started to feel ill. His wife is the one who reached out to Mamadou."

Mamadou had now joined them. He put his hand on the man's shoulder and spoke to him in his native tongue. Then he spoke in English, "I told him he is lucky you are here. That the medicine will work, and you will not report him."

Mansueki began to mumble incoherently. His eyes grew distant. Michael patted his hand. Mansueki's eyes traveled to Michael's hands, then to Michael's and Rachelle's faces. Cameron could see gratefulness in his expression, along with despair, shame, and exhaustion.

"Ask him if he knows who sent the other men?" Cameron was growing impatient.

Michael relayed the message, listened, then replied to Cameron. "All he knows is that they were armed, and they had the glasses to see in the dark. He doesn't know who gave them those things."

"There is only one group so advanced," Mamadou noted. "The one ran by the Golden Dragon." Mansueki's eyes widened at the mention of the name.

"Do you know who this Golden Dragon is?" Cameron asked Mansueki. "Do you know how to get in contact with him?"

Michael spoke with Mansueki again. "He does not. But he remembers the American was in a rush. Something about more tusks." Mansueki closed his eyes, then opened them slowly.

"Did they say where?" Cameron grew excited now.

"He's tired and must sleep." Rachelle glared at Cameron as she finished taping the new bandages. "The drugs will be kicking in."

Cameron got in close to the sick man; noses almost touching, Cameron tried not to grimace at Mansueki's rancid breath, which carried a hint of apple. "Try and remember. Anything else?"

Michael translated what Cameron had asked. Mansueki's eyes fluttered as he fought to keep them open.

Rachelle placed a hand on Cameron's shoulder and spoke softly, "He's tired. Let him sleep."

"If they are looking for more tusks, we don't have much time to figure this out, Rachelle." Cameron pinched the bridge of his nose with his fingers. "If we aren't too late already."

Chapter 12: No One Leaves Baby in the Car

The murmur of voices grew louder. Mac struggled to see in the dark of the new moon and could just make out the silhouettes of nearby brush shake and move in an oncoming pattern. Deep tones of conversation and laughter grew closer. *Sounds like men. How can they even see in this darkness,* she asked herself. A small group of shapes emerged from the brush.

It was several minutes before a spark of light cut through the darkness. *Good ... a fire.* Now Mac had no trouble seeing the five men. Mac noticed one had a large, plump sack, while the others carried sticks. *They must have been hunting.* They were near a hut, not far from where the Jeep was parked.

One man went into the hut, while the others pulled small shapes out from their sacks and laid them on a flat rock. When that was done, they began to cut into the dark shapes. She watched one of them heat a pot and put, what she could only guess was vegetables, in the water.

A stray dog shyly walked up. One of the men threw him something of what Mac was now sure was rat. In Africa, rat meat was not considered illegal bush meat, and always in good supply. As each slice of meat went into the pot, the idea that it was rat made her stomach flip.

The men looked in her direction. She slid lower in the seat, her eyes barely cresting the dashboard. They pointed. Mac wondered if they knew of the sick man in the hut or had noticed her slouched in the seat.

An unsettling wail of agony, not in English, came from the hut. The men turned, pointing and tilting their heads at each other, as if discussing who should go check on the occupant. Mac suspected, since the Jeep was by the hut's door, that they wouldn't—and no one did.

Another ten minutes went by. The smell of cooking rat had blown in her direction. The scent was like a dirty sock with a hint of piss.

Disgusting. If I wait here any longer, I'm going to be sick.

Mac opened the door slowly. She tried to shut it quietly, but the weight of the door made an audible *clunk.* The men stood in unison and looked at her. She instantly regretted her decision to leave the Jeep without grabbing the gun.

"It's okay, just here to see a sick friend," she said, waved, then walked briskly toward the hut's door.

Three of the men started to walk in her direction. She quickened her pace, glancing over her shoulder before knocking on the thin wooden door. The men stopped. Incoherent words passed between them, and she guessed the discussion was about her. Mac knocked harder and in a quickening tempo until she felt the door open.

Michael looked at her then past her in the direction of the men. "Is there trouble?"

"No, I ... was worried." Mac looked past Michael and saw a man on a bed. Rachelle looked to be securing a bright white bandage around his leg. In the corner, Mamadou was digging through the supplies.

"Everything okay?" Cameron walked up and stood beside Michael. His eyes quickly looked past Mac to the men behind her. His features stiffened and he stood straight. Mamadou joined them at the door. Seeing Mamadou, one of the men gave a weak wave, then they all returned to preparing their meal.

Cameron looked annoyed. "Better come in—did you bring the gun?"

"No. The smell of the rat was so bad I forgot." Mac's cheeks burned with embarrassment. "Do I need to go back and get it.?"

"No," Cameron told her.

"It doesn't smell much better in here." Michael took Mac's hand and led her inside. Mamadou returned to his boxes.

The injured man looked at her with bloodshot eyes. "Is he going to be okay?" Mac asked.

"He'll live," Rachelle stated in a monotone. She took out a bottle of pills, put them into Mansueki's hand, then gingerly closed his fist around them. "*Een elke vier uur*," she said to him. "One pill every four hours."

He nodded and patted her hand, holding onto for a second, before letting it slowly rest on his chest.

"He understood," Mamadou stated absently as he slid something from the supplies into his pocket.

Rachelle stood and pointed to the old bandages. "And burn those. Try not to touch them. I'll leave you some gloves to use to handle them." Mamadou nodded.

67

"Well, if you're done, Sherlock, I would like to get some sleep." Rachelle picked up her bag.

"Yes, I've got enough." Cameron reached to open the door.

"*Rooikop akkedis*." Mansueki pointed at Mac's hair.

"I'm really starting to take this personally," Mac replied dully.

"*Rooikop akkedis*," Mansueki said again, this time wiping at the top of his right arm.

"He's saying red lizard," Michael said quizzically. "I think he's referring to a tattoo."

Michael pointed to Cameron's tattoo. Mansueki nodded.

"Ask him if he means a red dragon or dinosaur." Cameron waited for Michael to translate. Mansueki nodded again and then began to explain something to Michael.

Michael translated while Mansueki spoke. "One of the men, big ... white, looked military. He had a tattoo that looked like a *likkewaan*. It's a big lizard around here. Nasty things. The tattoo is like that but ancient, with a red head and a bright orange eye."

"Well, that's something." Cameron looked at Mamadou. "Be sure to let me know if you have any more information."

Mamadou nodded.

Cameron turned to Rachelle and Michael. "Grab your stuff and let's get you to a bed to sleep in." He then placed his hands on Mac's arms and looked deeply into her eyes.

"Are you alright?" Cameron's voice was low and gentle. Mac was surprised by his tenderness and such intimacy in front of company.

"What? Yes. A little freaked out when the men started to follow me, but they were probably just concerned about their friend." She looked back at Mansueki. He was sleeping now, with a peaceful look upon his face, probably due to the drugs.

"I'm sorry I told you to wait. I should have just had you come in."

"Next time." Mac smiled.

"Let's hope not." Cameron chuckled, then placed his hand low on her back as he led her toward the door. His hand felt strong and good—safe. The intimate gesture didn't go unnoticed by Mac … or, by the look on her face, Rachelle.

Chapter 13: I'll Take Mine to Go

A black dome of night encased the bright streetlights of Mombasa. Gacoki drove through the busy streets toward his rendezvous. Honking, music, people laughing and talking filled the night. Pedestrians and street vendors crowded the sidewalks. The aroma of chapatis and beans flowed through his open window and his mouth watered. He passed a juice vendor and craved the sweet taste of sugar, lime, ginger, and mint of sugarcane juice. *No time to stop*, he told himself.

Gacoki maneuvered around the roundabout on Tangana Road then exited to his right on Moi Avenue. He effortlessly wove a white sedan through a sea of green, yellow, red, and blue tuk-tuks, a three-wheeled motorized taxi. Their whirring motors, combined with their massive numbers, made them look and sound like a locust swarm had invaded the streets of downtown.

In the distance stood the familiar giant aluminum elephant tusks that stretched over the lanes in a huge *M*. The tusks had been commissioned in commemoration of a 1952 visit to Mombasa by Queen Elizabeth II. Now, the sculpture was a tourist attraction. A drunken group stood on the median under the middle of the *M*. They held their cell phones up to capture a one-handed selfie to remember the moment.

"Stupid people," Gacoki told the small wiggling hula girl stuck to his car's dash. "They are taking a picture of metal in the shape of a letter." He gave the little hula girl a gentle flick so her tiny plastic hips would sway in agreement.

He drove by a section of white buildings with blue window frames. A tuk-tuk with a brown tarp door cut him off. He honked, cursing at the driver as he continued down the city center's main street to where the palm trees lining the medians stopped. At that point, he saw the restaurant he was instructed to go to. It had a small white sign painted with red letters that simply read: Chinese Restaurant.

He turned the sedan around the corner. The entrance was discreetly located at the back of the building. Gacoki parked, then walked quickly to the dimly lit door. He tried the handle; it was locked. Within seconds, the blinds on the door were whipped aside, and a very large Asian man looked down on him. Gacoki spotted the butt of a gun under his jacket.

"We are closed."

Gacoki recognized the man. It was Bai, from the docks.

"I am here to see the Dragon," Gacoki responded.

"What is your name?"

"Gacoki."

"Who sent you?"

"Idiot, I met you on the dock. Mr. Lin asked me to come. Do we all look alike? Forget me already?"

Bai frowned at the insult, then disappeared from the window. Gacoki heard the click and turn of a lock. The monster of a man opened the door with an emotionless expression.

"Go down the hall," he ordered, raising a meaty arm and pointing fingers that resembled sausages.

Gacoki did as he was told. He felt Bai's eyes on him as he followed him down the short hallway into the main seating area of the restaurant.

There were private booths and a handful of tables. Most of the clientele were Asian men. The women at the tables were likely prostitutes. He knew there were many restaurants in Africa that were operated by the Chinese, and Africans were either not welcome after 5 p.m. or not at all. He had a sinking feeling he had just walked into one.

Bai guided him to a private booth. Chen's other bodyguard, Jiang, stood close by. Chen was hard to miss. He was the only Asian in the room with dyed blond streaks in his dark hair. He reminded Gacoki of a polecat.

"Ah. It's the Kenyan." Chen made no effort to stand or offer for Gacoki to sit.

A waitress, in a traditional Chinese pink cheongsam dress, daintily stepped up and placed a black tokkuri bottle and two matching ochoko cups on the table. Chen poured clear liquid in the cups, then passed one to Gacoki.

"It's saké. It has become quite popular in China." Chen picked up his cup and held it to his nose. Gacoki watched as Chen took a deep breath then a small sip, which he visibly didn't swallow for a few seconds. Gacoki mimicked him. It tasted of nuts and cinnamon, followed by the bitterness of alcohol.

"I didn't expect you here," Gacoki stated looking down.

"I take it you were expecting the Dragon. I hope you are not disappointed with my company." Chen swallowed the second half of his drink, poured himself another, then topped off Gacoki's.

Gacoki had expected to see the Dragon and was disappointed to be standing across from this fool. "Of course not. Pleasure to see you again," he lied. He sipped his drink, then held the cup close so it wouldn't be filled again. He wanted all his wits about him.

Chen continued, "The Dragon has a job for you. You do this right and who knows … maybe you will get to see him."

"What's the job?"

Three wait staff interrupted the meeting with several plates of food. Gacoki had never seen so much variety. There was fried rice, noodles, egg rolls, chicken with cashews, and fried prawns. He hated that it smelled wonderful. He hated this man and everything about him. He didn't want to like anything about Chen or what he touched.

"Ah, finally." Chen picked up a serving spoon, then moved food to his bowl before diving in with his chopsticks. Gacoki's mouth watered.

"Here's what I need you to do." Chen took a bite, chewed, and swallowed. "You need to deliver two thousand and seven hundred kilos of ivory to the Port of Mombasa."

"You've got to be mad. That's almost two hundred tusks."

"I'm not expecting you to go out and kill them. I doubt you would find that many. What I'm expecting is for you to move them to the cargo ship."

"How did you even get that much?"

"I have several men, just like yourself. They have been gathering the ivory for me for a while in several locations. Some straight out of a police warehouse."

"And you trust these people?" Gacoki looked at Chen, who started laughing.

"Of course, I don't. That's why I'm sending you to get it." Chen filled his cup and swallowed the saké quickly this time.

"So, I'm your pawn?" Gacoki growled.

"Don't take it so personal. Consider it an initiation. You do this for me, and I give you more and better work. Soon, you'll be making decent money while some other new guy takes all the risk."

"And how do you plan on hiding that many elephant tusks? They will know to investigate crates."

"I'm not using crates," Chen explained. "I have modified containers with false compartments in the back. The last three feet of the container are false, and the majority of the container will be filled with timber. I've been able to get three tons of cargo on these forty-foot containers to Hong Kong in the past. I have two containers, just in case. All you need to do is get the cargo to the dock. I'll have the containers waiting. You'll be in and out."

Chen placed more food on his plate. "Besides, you won't be alone. You'll meet up with one of my men."

"I don't need help." Gacoki frowned at Chen but could see that the option to work alone was not up for negotiation. *This will complicate things.*

Chen smiled. "He's an ex-military badass, and one of my best. He's also going to pay the contact."

"How will I know him?"

"You can't miss him," Chen mumbled then took three big bites of noodles. Gacoki waited impatiently. Chen swallowed and continued, "One of *the* best hunters and trackers for hire. He's on his way. He had a supply issue to deal with. Jiang, come and give Gacoki the location." Chen made a slight beckoning motion with his chopsticks.

Gacoki almost jumped when Jiang's small frame appeared in his peripheral vision. Jiang handed him the list.

"You remember Jiang?" Chen pointed with his chopsticks.

"Of course. I never forget a face." *Especially ugly faces*, he thought to himself. Jiang's expression was so emotionless that he gave Gacoki the creeps.

"Ah, there's our friend now." Chen waved.

From the corner of the restaurant, a tall light brown skinned man walked toward the table. His dark olive bush shirt and khaki pants should have made him inconspicuous, except his model good looks, angled cheek bones and square jaw, made him stand out in any crowd.

Gacoki felt dwarfed next to the man, whose sleeves were rolled-up high to reveal a tattoo of an ugly, orange-eyed red lizard. Unlike him, the new man was invited to sit beside Chen.

"This is Jacob. Jacob, Gacoki." Chen pointed at each with his chopsticks. They both nodded to each other.

The waitress, with a younger woman beside her, quickly arrived with a plate for Jacob. The younger woman looked at Jacob then dipped her gaze down while giggling.

"Saké?" she offered in a small voice. She set down a small cup for him then picked up the tokkuri.

"Don't mind if I do." Jacob picked up the cup, his large hand dwarfed it like a giant at a tea party. With his elbow on the table, he leaned in closer to her, as if looking for a kiss. "How could I resist from such a beauty?" Jacob flashed a smile showing perfectly straight white teeth. The young woman giggled again and poured his drink, then the two women quickly left.

"Do you always have that effect on women?" Chen asked Jacob.

"Yes. Even the gay ones." Jacob and Chen snorted. Gacoki wasn't in the mood for jokes. He also didn't miss the fact that Jacob was held in a higher regard; an equal.

"How much am I getting?" Gacoki blurted, tired of playing games.

"You get two thousand American dollars," Chen answered with a smile.

"Do you take me for a fool?" Gacoki placed his hands on the table and leaned in. Chen and Jacob calmly looked at him. Jiang and Bai stepped closer to the table.

"How much is your American friend getting?" Gacoki tipped his chin at Jacob.

Jacob spun noodles around his chopsticks and started to eat. "You're being rude and causing a scene," he said between chews. "If they throw you out, we're done doing business."

Gacoki took a step back. Bai and Jiang faded into the background just as quickly as they had arrived.

"I suggest you worry about yourself for now— I'm an honorable businessman." Chen leaned back, another drink in his hand.

"My people get cheated all the time. They get lied to and stolen from. I want seven thousand."

"Can you believe this guy?" Chen addressed Jacob. Jacob only shrugged while he sipped his saké and stabbed an eggroll with his chopstick.

I know my price isn't even one percent of what Chen stand to make. These smugglers run on the blood of my people, and I'm going to make them all pay for the death of my father.

"Two thousand is more than you'll make in months." Chen raised his eyebrows, his smile stretching across his face, making him look like a snake. "And you're just picking up and delivering. It's not like you hunted them down yourself."

"Yes, but if I get caught ... such a sizable amount will come with great penalty."

"Three," Chen countered.

"Six and a half," Gacoki stated flatly.

"Four."

"Six." Gacoki stared at Chen. Chen's eyes didn't leave his nor did he make any other movements.

"I think you have done this more than I assumed. I'll give you three now and two and a half upon drop off, but if you miss any of the locations, no second payment."

"Deal," Gacoki relented. Chen gave a nod in the direction of Jiang. Jiang disappeared from the room then came back with an envelope. Gacoki reached for it.

"Don't insult me by counting it here," Chen cautioned.

Gacoki discreetly put it in his pocket.

The waitress returned, only to have Chen waved her away.

"Jacob will meet you at the three locations listed in the envelope. Pick up everything and drive straight to Kilindini Harbour. The goods must arrive between midnight and 1 a.m. at the ship named *Floating Orchid*. I have men who will make sure it gets on the boat, but you must make that window. It will be tight."

"Understood."

"Now … business is done."

Gacoki took that as his hint to leave. He would have like to have reached across the table and strangle Chen.

Chen is just a pawn, he mused. He wanted the boss, the Dragon himself. *I'll have to play the game until I can work my way up in ranks. I will have my revenge soon.*

Chapter 14: Silent Night

A weak cheer rose from the battered and tired group as Cameron pulled up to the guest sleeping quarters at the ranch. It was well into night, and everyone wanted nothing more than to sleep.

A big yawn and a groan came from Michael. "I need to get some serious z's on something that isn't moving. I would take a floor right now if you offered it."

"After a good night's sleep and breakfast, I'll take you back to your camp. Rachelle, do you need to check in if you don't go back tonight?"

"No. I took care of everything before we left. And I'm going to agree with Michael. Some real sleep would be nice."

Mac dwelled upon Mansueki, the man back in the hut, how he was sleeping on something she wouldn't consider comfortable for a dog. The pain medicine at least lessened the pain. She pitied him. She shouldn't, because of the elephant he helped slaughter, but she did.

"There are two guest rooms reserved for special visitors." Cameron pointed to their right. "I think, after today, you qualify. You should find them more than comfortable. You'll even have real showers in the rooms. Water pressure isn't great, but it'll clean you off before bed."

"Awesome, thanks man." Michael gave Cameron a weak fist bump.

"I need to drop Mac off at her quarters. You both were amazing back there. Thank you for your help."

Rachelle touched Cameron's shoulder before getting out of the Jeep. "So were you."

There's that look again. They still have a connection.

The two tiredly shuffled towards their rooms, clothes wrinkled, hair a mess.

"They look like two medical Zombies," Mac commented quietly, and Cameron chuckled.

Minutes later, Cameron stopped at Mac's bungalow door. She could hardly keep her eyes open.

"Curbside service." He was back to the playful Cameron she was used to and not the serious secret ops guy she had just spent the last several hours with.

"Thanks." Mac turned and opened her door. She was half out when Cameron grabbed her hand, stopping her from leaving entirely. She looked down at their hands. He was holding hers softly. She raised her gaze to meet Cameron's coppery eyes.

"I'm sorry about today. I was worried about you. I put you in too much danger back there when I left you in the car. I don't know what I would do if you got hurt on my watch."

"I'm not helpless." Mac frowned. "I *can* help."

"I know." He dropped his gaze to their intertwined hands, as if he had to summon courage to continue. "Whatever happened between me and Rachelle ... it happened a long time ago," Cameron blurted.

"Why are you telling me this?" Mac was taken off guard at the outburst. *I don't think everything is in the past.*

"Red, I care about you. Maybe more than I should, considering our situation."

Mac's heart beat faster and her stomach dropped, like she was on a roller coaster.

"What *is* our situation?"

Cameron looked at her for what seemed a long time. Then he pulled her back into the Jeep and kissed her. One hand still holding hers, he stroked her face with the other. It was a soft, full kiss, and she felt it all over. His warm lips tasted sweet and salty.

When he slowly pulled away, a very real part of her did not want him to.

"I ... that was nice," was all she managed to say, her cheeks instantly feeling hot.

He gently tucked a piece of her hair behind her ear. "Get some sleep, Red. I'll see you tomorrow."

Chapter 15: Kiss and Run

How could he just kiss me like that then drive away? Mac walked to her bungalow in a daze. She peeked out her window and was happy to see the Jeep headed to his quarters and not back to Rachelle's.

A high pitch bark sounded from inside the bungalow. *Fenny's probably missing me, and I forgot to ask Lebron to feed him. Of course, I didn't expect to be gone so long either.* Upon opening the door, Fenny's barks turned into high-pitched happy screams, which sounded more like a small monkey than a fox. She walked over and let him out of his pen. He circled her feet, darted quickly around the room several times, then hid under the bed.

She had brought, or rather appropriated, him from JAWS, the Josephine Animal Welfare Sanctuary, in Kerrville Texas, where she had worked before coming to Africa. The Fennec foxes' tiny frame and bat-like ears made them look adorable more than menacing. But owners, like Fenny's, soon found out that these high-energy, exotic, nocturnal mammals were loud and quite a handful.

Mac didn't agree with people having fennec foxes as pets, but Fenny had been surrendered to the rescue already tame and unable to be released into the wild. Mac and her late fiancé would sneak in his pen at night and play with him. When she left the sanctuary, she couldn't bear the idea of no one playing with him and feared he may die of loneliness—so she took him.

Or maybe she took him because he was the last thing that reminded her of Keene. Maybe both.

"I'm a little confused, Fenny." Mac walked over to a jar of crickets then picked one out for Fenny. As she let the cricket go, he bounded toward it. The hunt was on, and Fenny was up to the challenge. Mac walked pass her bed, with longing eyes, to her long wood-framed mirror. "I like Cameron, but I miss Keene so much," she told her reflection, since Fenny seemed disinterested in matters of the heart.

From underneath her shirt, she pulled out a ring that hung around her neck on a long silver chain. The ring was adorned with a circle of elephants, a gift that Keene was never able to give her. His uncle gave it to her. That was when she'd found out he had planned to propose. A proposal she was never able to hear. It hurt her heart to think about it. She clenched the ring in her fist, as if that would settle her mind.

I like Cameron ... I'm attracted to him ... but I still miss Keene. I mean, do I like him? Or am I just lonely.

She pulled off her sweaty shirt and dropped her khakis to her feet, flipping them across the room with her toes. She whipped her white cotton bra off with ninja speed and *ahh'd* at the freedom from the tight elastic. She tugged on an oversized pink shirt and looked at her image in the mirror. Sweaty hair clung to her face. In the States, she kept her hair pixie short and spiked. Here, she didn't have time to care for it as much, so she kept it longer, long enough for a ponytail.

She ran her fingers thru it. *Cameron once mentioned he liked my hair longer,* she thought absently.

She flopped on her bed. Fenny, apparently full of cricket, jumped up and snuggled on her lap. She tried to process the day—the dead elephant, the market, and the wounded man. But the image of Cameron and how his lips felt tumbled around her head like a clothes dryer.

As Mac felt sleep finally take over, one last thought crossed her mind ... *I wonder if Rachelle would be jealous?*

Chapter 16: Where's My Coffee

The low glow of the Micky Mouse clock on the dresser showed her it was 5:30 a.m., an hour before the sun would rise. Mac yearned to sleep more, only her inner timeclock was on a strict schedule and her body wouldn't let her. Even if she wasn't early to bed, she was always early to rise.

Fenny's tiny body was warm on her feet. Like a mother to her child, she watched as his light golden fur rose and fell with each breath. His pointed ears were laid back as his muzzle rested contently on his favorite toy; a ratty old stuffed mouse Mac had sewn from an old blue sock of hers.

Mac closed her eyes in hopes she could convince her body it wasn't time to get up. Details from the previous day spun through her head like a ball on a roulette wheel, settling on the memory of Cameron's warm lips and his last words, 'I care about you, maybe more than I should'. This woke her up quicker than an espresso.

What the heck was that supposed to mean? She scrunched up her face like a toddler eating a lemon.

The first thing she wanted to do, of course, was to find Cameron. A more rational plan of action was to smell better and to get caffeinated. She gave her toes a slight wriggle. Fenny opened his little black eyes, stared at her for a second, then bounded to the floor, his nails clacking in rapid succession as he circled the bed while barking excitedly.

"I'm up. I'm up. You'll get your breakfast." She swung her feet to the floor. The wood was smooth and cool, with the air around her bordering on muggy. The vintage oscillating fan in her room rotated warm air through squeaky metal blades and gave little reprive to the heat. She glanced at a calendar on the wall, she couldn't believe it was Saturday already.

Mac plucked a cricket from the glass jar and put it on the floor.

"I'll bring you back something from breakfast."

Fenny paid her no attention. He had a cricket to murder.

Due to Chimp's wealth, the three volunteer huts had access to a well and generator-powered electric pumps, providing running water to the bungalows so that they had their own showers. The ranger huts down the road had community showers. All the showers had only cold water, but she was grateful for the running water instead of having to trek to the river, as did most people in the Congo region.

Mac stripped and prepared herself for a quick shower. Cool water ran over her. It felt good to scrub her scalp and body, washing away the remanence of yesterday with lavender and vanilla suds. She figured she probably should have taken a shower last night instead of stinking up her bed. However, exhaustion had taken precedence over cleanliness.

After her shower, Mac looked in her small closet. She had little to choose from, so she opted for the plain blue V-neck shirt and brown khaki shorts. She dressed quickly, then laced up her working boots, then pulled her hair into a short ponytail.

"Well, Fenny, what do you think? Beauty regimen complete?" Fenny had a mouthful of grasshopper and crunched on it excitedly.

"I'll take that as a resounding yes. Now get in your cage." She plucked two more crickets from the jar and put them in his cage. Fenny ran in, the twitching legs of his first hunting success sticking out from his mouth. He happily searched for the other two, trying to catch them before they found their way out. She locked the cage.

"Let's go see if there's coffee and find out what the Cameron situation is. Did I mention he kissed me?"

His words, *'I care about you, maybe more than I should, considering our situation,'* resonated in her head again. That wasn't a romantic movie line. It was a statement from a man who had lived a life and already had his roadblocks set out in front of him.

Mac sighed as she went out the door. The only thing she knew for certain was that she needed coffee.

***

Mac was almost at the kitchen when she spotted Cameron and a thin, balding, older man with a stark white goatee walking out from the command center. They looked to be crossing to the kitchen as well.

"Good morning," she called out and waved energetically. *Way to play it cool*, she told herself.

"Red," answered Cameron. "Good morning. This is my friend and the owner of this ranch, Chimp O'Neilson." The two men waited for her to catch up.

"Hi! I'm Mac."

"Good morning, young lady," the man spoke in a grandfatherly tone and held out his hand. Mac grasped it, and he shook it excitedly, placing his other hand over the top of hers. "I have heard such good things about the work you have done … with the baby elephants. I'm sorry it has taken me so long to meet you. I've been tied up with … with business. We're so lucky to have you."

She blushed at the compliment. Chimp's eyes stayed focused on her. They were a bright golden brown, floating in a sea of wrinkles, as if a young man's soul was trapped in an older man's body.

"Thank you. In all honesty, it doesn't feel like enough and I wish I could do more."

"Nonsense. You've done more already. You're here." Chimp held out his hands displaying the land around him. Mac couldn't help but smile. He was charming.

"I was just asking this handsome young man about our guests." He patted Cameron on the back. "I heard you all had an exciting night, last night." His statement sounded as if they had all gone bowling.

"That's what I like about you, Chimp," Cameron remarked. "Nothing really phases you as dangerous."

"Was it dangerous?" Chimp asked.

"No, I suppose it really wasn't."

Mac was surprised at Cameron's response. She remembered all the men around the fire and how they had looked at her.

"It might have been a little dangerous," she answered, placing her thumb and index finger slightly apart.

"Anyway, my boy— you were saying before the lovely Miss Mac joined us that you think you have a lead."

Cameron looked around. "Mind going somewhere private?"

"Come, let's go to my quarters. You can join us, Mac. Cameron has assured me of your trustworthiness."

Mac chanced a glance at Cameron who smiled briefly and winked. Butterflies erupted in her stomach, as well as a pang of guilt. Mac followed the pair to Chimp's quarters, a place she had never been in. This was the first time she saw the door open and surmised that it must be kept locked when Chimp was away.

Chimp led them into a beautiful sitting room with several box seats topped by plush deep red cushions. The room was decorated with tribal masks, woven rugs, and wooden statues of elephants, gods, and voodoo-looking figures. The entire back of the room was open and looked out onto the property.

"I have something to tell you as well, Cameron," Chimp announced.

"Are you okay?" Cameron pointed at Chimp's stomach. "It looks like you've lost a lot of weight. You on one of those fad diets?"

"No, just age and gravity winning against time. You'll see. There will be a day when the ladies don't swoon over you. But not now, right." Chimp winked at Mac, and she rolled her eyes and smiled in reply.

"At least I'm rich," Chimp continued. "That keeps them way past the time the looks disappear."

"I guess I should start saving then," Cameron responded. Chimp chuckled softly, waving his hand as if money should be the least of his worries.

Chimp pushed a button on the wall. Cool air and a stale, metallic smell instantly poured around them.

"Air conditioning?" Mac enjoyed the feel of an almost cold breeze.

"Not air conditioning. Just a fan made in this decade. Please sit." Chimp gestured toward the chairs.

The cushions made loud *whoomph* sounds as they sat. They laughed at the gaseous noise.

"You go first." Chimp pointed at Cameron. "Seems you had more excitement than I." He leaned forward, his attention fully focused on Cameron.

"I know there were five men on the property. One was a hired local. He had gotten hurt. One—probably prior military—a white guy with a tattoo of what they called an ancient lizard. I'm guessing a dinosaur. The others didn't seem local and had guns and advanced military gear, like night-vision goggles."

Chimp nodded as Cameron continued, "Also, I'm sure they're the ones who killed the bull elephant in the park the other day. Which means they'll be back. If they've gotten that far in, then they've probably seen the tracks to our herd. Your turn, Chimp."

Chimp clasped his hands and tapped his lips in a look of contemplations before answering. "I received word from one of my dearest friends, Kendalie, that he suspects there's a spy somewhere in our group."

Cameron's eyebrows furrowed as he grimaced. Mac stiffened at the word "spy." She envisioned a Cold War persona, someone wearing a long trench coat and a brown fedora.

"That would explain why the poachers seemed to be one step ahead all the time," she remarked.

"Do either of you have any ideas about who the spy in our midst might be? If there is one." Chimp looked to Mac.

"Maybe Abebe has an idea?" She shrugged.

He then looked at Cameron, who paused before shaking his head side to side.

"I think he would have confided in me if he did," Cameron remarked tersely.

"Don't be so sure," Chimp added. "Remember, the African Apartheid made laws that divided racial groups. It was a social system that severely disadvantaged most of the population, especially the "non-white". There is a deep seeded suspicion between the races due to the segregation and unfair laws of the past that will take many more decades to heal. If African's are doing anything illegal or wrong, they will not report it to white people. There is no trust there."

Cameron answered confidently, "I'll ask Abebe. I know he would tell me."

Mac asked Chimp, "How do you know your friend Kendalie isn't the mole?"

"We have shared many secrets." Chimp placed his index finger in front of his lips and smiled secretively. "We know where each other's skeletons are buried."

"How do you know it's not me or Mac?" Cameron asked and Mac involuntarily snorted at the idea. Then became embarrassed when she realized he was asking a serious question.

The men stared at each other, unblinking before Chimp finally answered, "My gut. My circle of trust is small. Cameron, Kendalie, and now Mac because you trust her, Cameron. Which brings me to the other reason that I'm here." Mac noticed a sadness in Chimp's eyes. "If something happens to me, the ranch is set up as a nonprofit. Cameron, I'll need you to stay on and run it. Not forever, if you don't want to, but at least until you name another who will take care of it and the elephants."

"I'm honored." Cameron sat up straighter. "Is there something you're not telling me?"

Chimp waved him off. "Just being responsible and having a will, something normal at my age. I also need to ensure the wildlife on my property will continue to be safe. I fought too many years to save the wildlife of Africa; it would be irresponsible of me if I did not build a system that could sustain itself way past my lifetime. I'm still not sure what to do with the family home ... so many memories ... and it has been in our family for generations."

Mac found this statement foreboding. If Cameron felt the same, he didn't show it.

"I'll see this ranch is taken care of. I know how much it means to you and to the animals that call it home."

Chimp smiled, placed his hands on his knees, then stood abruptly. "Enough of all this. Let me meet your other friends. I'm sure Mac is starving. I can hear her stomach from here. Mustn't keep a lady waiting or hungry."

Chapter 17: Chimp and Friends

In the dining area, Mac was surprised to see Michael and Rachelle already sitting at the table and eating.

"I figured you would sleep in," Mac addressed the pair. Michael's hair was messy, and his arms were curled around a bowl of food while he chewed slowly. Rachelle, on the other hand, was freshly showered with her blond hair pulled back in a tight ponytail. She was a natural beauty.

"I've not slept past 6 a.m. in two decades," Rachelle responded as she sipped on her coffee.

"*Mm-hmm*, Corinne's a genius," Michael mumbled through a mouthful of food as he waved Mac, Cameron, and Chimp over with his free hand. "This was worth waking up for."

Mac looked at the unusually fruitful bounty and assumed it was laid out due to Chimp's presence. There were bananas, pineapples, dates, figs, olives, and oranges, along with thick sausages, toast, jams, and tea.

"You should visit more often, Chimp," Mac exclaimed as she sat at the table. "This is quite a spread."

Corinne bustled out of the kitchen, with what looked like an expensive China teapot and cup. "Good morning, Mr. O'Neilson." Corinne sang the words.

"Good morning, Corinne. What a delightful breakfast you've made for us."

Mac had to remind herself that even though Cameron and Chimp acted casual, Chimp's visit was a big deal. She was in the presence of a rich and influential man.

"It was no trouble at all, Luv," Corinne sang. "Please sit. I have your PG Tips steeped nice and strong. Managed to get you some nice fresh milk as well." Corinne seemed to float to Chimp's side, then she poured him a *cuppa*, as she often referred to tea.

"Thank you, Corinne." Chimp flashed her a smile, causing Corinne to blush. Mac found the exchange endearing.

Chimp was charming, and they were of the same age range, plus he was a passionate, powerful, and seemingly kind man—women's catnip. *This is probably what Keene would have grown into if he had lived to that age*. The idea saddened Mac. It was sometimes hard to live a life that was the opposite of what you had planned and without the someone you had planned it with.

"Miss Mac, are you alright?" Chimp's soft brown eyes were focused on her.

"Oh, um, well … you just reminded me of someone I lost," Mac's voice cracked a little. "I believe he would have been a great animal advocate, like you." She rarely mentioned Keene. It was too painful. And though time had helped, there were still moments that overwhelmed her.

She knew Cameron was looking at her but didn't want to look at him.

"I'm sorry for your loss, and I'm humbled that you could draw a comparison." Chimp reached across the table and patted Mac's hand. The gesture made the tears she'd been fighting flow from her eyes. He continued, "Sometimes, when we lose someone special, it's better to not focus on what they could have been but to reflect on how their life and sacrifices helped those they left behind. I know all about you, Mac. You've done a lot of good here. I'm sure your special someone would be proud of you." Chimp released her hand and took a sip of tea.

"Amen," Cameron added.

"I couldn't agree more." Rachelle held out a hand. "I'm—"

"Rachelle McDonald," Chimp exclaimed and shook Rachelle's hand. "And you're Michael Barren," he stated after disengaging from Rachelle.

Michael wiped the juice from the orange he was eating on his pants before taking Chimp's outstretched hand. "Nice to meet you."

"Cameron speaks well of you both. I admire your service to the people of Africa. Cameron tells me, Rachelle, that you both served together."

As she tried to regain her composure, Mac was relieved the subject matter had shifted from her.

"Yes, we did," Rachelle stated and seemed a little astonished. Mac was also surprised Chimp knew about the company at the table. It was probably one of the reasons he was such a success.

Rachelle elaborated, "I was in the Air Force stationed at Al Dhafra Air Base in the United Arab Emirates. Medical, obviously, and Cameron was on special duty. He was flown in for a TDY when the base was under threat. Kind of like the cavalry. He was on a one-hundred-and-eighty-day vacation at the expense of the United States." Rachelle smiled.

"Vacation ... right," Cameron added. "Uncle Sam makes a crappy travel agent."

"So how did you meet?" Chimp prodded. "I'm sure there's a story there."

Rachelle and Cameron made eye contact, then snickered in a way that made Mac a little jealous. However, Chimp looked positively giddy with anticipation.

"Oh, you're going to love this," Michael stated while leaning back and patting his full belly. "I know the story well but love hearing it."

Mac noted that Rachelle must talk a lot about Cameron.

"Right." Rachelle clicked her tongue. "Back at the base, there were tons of stray cats, all quite friendly and great pest control. However, they were also good carriers of rabies, which was a pretty common problem over there with all the stray cats and dogs. This guy," Rachelle tilted her head in Cameron's direction, "being the animal softy he is ... adopted practically an entire colony of cats and fed them against the commander's orders."

"In my defense," Cameron held up his hands in a surrender gesture, "I was doing just fine until One-Eyed Joe."

"One-Eyed Joe?" Mac laughed.

"Ah yes, One-Eyed Joe. He was the cutest, most beautiful one-eyed cat you've ever seen," Rachelle sighed. "Gray luxurious fur and only one bright blue eye. Anyway, Mr. Marine got himself bit and ended up in my office."

"That cat was psycho. Rubbing against my leg and begging for a pet one minute and then chomp!" Cameron made an alligator hand gesture to mimic the bite.

"Four doses of rabies vaccine later . . ." Rachelle shrugged.

"That stuff sucked." Cameron picked up the story. The volley of storytelling between them was effortless, like a practiced comedy duo. "I was confined to quarters for three days with the side effects. And we didn't even know if the cat had rabies. I wouldn't have even gone to the clinic, except some rule-following Staff Sergeant tattled."

"Well, that sergeant might have saved your life. Anyway. I ended up having to check on him."

"A regular Florence Nightingale," Michael added. Cameron and Rachelle looked at each other.

There is that connection again, Mac's inner voice told her.

"That was the start of us dating." Rachelle raised her index finger. "But more importantly, it made that place a little more bearable. I don't know what I would have done without Cameron. He helped me through some rough crap, professional and personal. The military is not always an easy place for women. Especially, women in charge."

"Remember that jerk Tech Sergeant?" Cameron snapped his fingers. "Matt! That was his name," Cameron exclaimed shaking his head in disapproval.

"The one who kept putting his hand on my knee?" Rachelle shuddered. "Yeah, I remember him."

"What happened to him?" Mac, even if she was a little jealous, was completely enthralled with their past.

"Oh, I told Cameron about him. One day and one black eye later, Technical Sergeant Creepy never put a hand on my knee again."

"You didn't get in trouble?" Mac asked Cameron.

"Nah, he knew that if he told on me, I would be back. And if I told on him, he would lose a stripe. So, it was win-win, as far as I was concerned." Cameron paused and looked at Rachelle. "I mean, I knew Rachelle could take care of herself, but I was sure it wasn't that dude's first time doing something like that. I wanted to make sure it was his last."

"Good for you," Chimp exclaimed and clapped Cameron's back.

"Good thing the cat bit you," Mac added. "Otherwise, that creep would have never gotten his comeuppance."

"Yep. Way to go ol' One-Eye." Rachelle sipped her coffee. "We should head back soon. Michael and I have a lot to do. We have to move camp. Which is a shame. I've gotten attached to those kids."

"If you'll excuse me, I must be on my way too." Chimp stood. Cameron and the others stood in unison, so Mac took her cue and stood. "I've enjoyed this conversation, but I must also get to work. Rachelle, Michael, have a safe journey." He shook their hands again. "Cameron and Mac, stay safe and I'll see you soon."

Chimp left and they all sat back down.

"Well, you heard the man," Cameron stated to the group. "That's our cue to get going. If everyone's finished with breakfast, we could leave in fifteen."

"That works for me." Michael stretched then picked up four sausages. "For the road," he stated with a sheepish smile and a fist full of meat.

"I'll be ready," Rachelle replied.

"You guys have a safe trip." Mac stood to shake their hands.

"You aren't going?" Cameron asked.

"I don't think you need me. Plus, I should get ready for Amahle's birth … just in case." Mac took some olives, figs, and orange slices put them in her napkin. "For Fenny." Mac lied and filled another napkin full of food and quickly walked out the door.

***

Mac was sneaking food for Labron. She had been doing it on and off for months. He would love the goodies today. She also had been worried about Labron since she witnessed Siyabonga scolding him the other day. She walked quickly to the lobby. Lebron was sitting at the front desk, looking bored until he saw her and her very full napkin. His face lit up.

"Miss Mac! Is that for me?"

"Yes, and it's good stuff." Mac handed Lebron the napkins.

"Oh, thank you, Miss Mac." Lebron opened a napkin, his eyes widened at the food as he quickly started to pop the nuts into his mouth.

"Lebron, were you okay the other day? It looked like Siyabonga was … well, it looked like you were in trouble."

Lebron cast his eyes down and focused on the food. "Yes, Miss. He was looking at my papers."

"What papers?"

Lebron shrugged, turned over the food, and inspected it too seriously. Mac figured she must have touched upon a sore issue.

"Sorry to pry. Just checking up on my friend."

Lebron looked up at her and smiled. There was something different, something sad about his smile, like a kid who got praise for a test he knew he cheated on. "Thank you for the food," he said again softly with his eyes looking at the floor.

"If you need to talk, Lebron, don't be afraid to."

She didn't know what was wrong and could feel he wanted to tell her something. And that something probably had to with Siyabonga. "Is it about—"

Cameron walked in.

"You are going to want to join us," he stated matter-of-factly.

"Why?" Mac asked. *I can't think of any reason to endure another car ride.*

"Oupa and his family have been sighted."

Damn. Nothing except that.

Chapter 18: Why Did the Gorilla Cross the Road?

A morning mist offered a protective shroud over the park's inhabitants. The haze seemed to grip the trees, resting below the tree line. Temperatures were beginning their quick climb to the nineties, which meant it would dissipate soon. Mac hoped to be back at the ranch by midday, so she could check on the herd. She especially wanted to see if Amahle was showing signs of labor. But she couldn't pass up a chance to see Oupa and his family of gorillas; they had been elusive these last few weeks.

"Your three o'clock," Cameron shouted over his shoulder. A herd of grazing antelope raised their heads one by one as they passed.

"That's amazing," Rachelle shouted over the noise of the engine.

While nearing one of the water crossings, a wall of bright green, gray, and orange filled the air.

"Cool," Michael exclaimed. He was looking in every direction as a massive flock of birds took flight before the Jeep's path then quickly descended after they passed. "What are they?"

"Those are treron calvus," Cameron yelled.

"Sounds exotic," Rachelle replied.

Mac giggled.

"What?" Rachelle gave a perplexed look.

"They're pigeons," Mac grinned.

"They're too beautiful to just call them pigeons," Cameron remarked.

The Jeep slowed as they came to a stop.

"What? What is it?" Mac asked expectedly. She, Rachelle, and Michael quickly scanned around them.

"Over there," Cameron whispered and pointed to a line of trees.

Several black figures were gathered at the base of a large tree. Some were in the tree's branches.

"I don't—" Rachelle gasped. "I've never seen gorillas in the wild. This is amazing!"

"That is Oupa." She pointed to the largest gorilla. He was up on all fours. His silver hair blanketed his back. "I can't see everyone. There are seven family members."

"Eight, hopefully," Cameron added. "I received word this morning that Natala gave birth. Probably happened a few weeks ago; the little one was just spotted. Newborns are so tiny, and gorillas don't show like humans. Sometimes we get a nice surprise when a new family member is added."

"That's exciting!" Mac turned to Michael. "Not only is a baby good news ... it means the gorillas feel safe enough to procreate."

"I know I like to feel safe when I procreate," Michael joked then blushed. "Sorry, I'm in mixed company."

The all quietly snickered. Mac was beginning to think of them as her friends.

"Oh, here he comes to check us out," Cameron whispered. "Everyone, stay still." He leaned over the steering wheel, as if to shrink his size.

"I can see him," Rachelle's voice was barely audible.

All Michael could manage to say was "Wow." His mouth hung open in awe.

Oupa strutted out from the trees. Though he was far away, his massive size was impressive. Unafraid, he stared at the Jeep as if investigating why the vehicle had stopped. Without words, his stance and face passed the message that he would do anything to keep his family safe if necessary.

"I have goose bumps," Rachelle whispered.

"I have goose bumps on my goose bumps," Michael added.

Mac smile and thought how lucky she was to be here seeing such animals in the wild. Most people would only be able to glimpse these beautiful creatures caged at zoos or parks.

"It's crazy to think our generation may be the last to see these animals in the wild," Mac spoke low, looking at the great silverback.

"What?" Michael looked at her. "Really?"

"Yes, natural parks are about the only safe places from poaching and land encroachment. When there are no more animals outside the parks, the poachers will go into the parks. The government is slow, and funding relies heavily on world involvement. It's a huge undertaking that all countries need to be involved in."

"Not to mention the corruption," Cameron added. "There's always someone, somewhere, trying to take what they can, when they can, and at all costs."

"I didn't understand it in the past," Rachelle stated looking at Cameron, "but I get now why you had to come here and do this." Their eyes settled on each other, exchanging a look of sadness, understanding, and even closure.

After a few minutes of silence, Oupa picked at the vegetation around him and ate. Seeing his action as a sign of safety, more family members emerged from the tree line. The female gorillas tended to the younger ones, who played like human children; running around each other and occasionally annoying the adults.

A tear fell from Michael's eye as the Jeep slowly rolled away from the family. "Thank you so much for stopping." He took a cloth from his pocket and wiped his face. "I'll remember this forever."

Chapter 19: Back at Camp

The camp was already bustling with activity when they arrived. The line of patients looked like yesterdays; women were with their children, most of the children didn't have shoes, and too many of the children were rail thin. The stone-faced children disturbed her the most. What had these children faced that took away their smiles, innocence, and happiness from their hearts so soon?

Cameron parked in front of the main tent. There was a long pause where no one moved or uttered a word ... just looked at the camp. It was a lot to take in. From a nature-rich ranch to a camp full of poor, malnourished children, the difference was night and day.

"It breaks my heart to see them so young and sad." Mac looked at Rachelle. "Are they all here for vaccines?"

"Vaccines or they are sick. We also provide emergency food aid, maternal care, mental health services, and HIV prevention and treatment services. Sadly, HIV is a serious issue here." Rachelle sighed as she scanned the sea of children. "Without the proper treatments, pregnant mothers can pass the infection to their babies. Young girls also have a high risk of infection due to early marriage and sometimes abuse. We're hoping to stop this vicious cycle. Just like you, we're trying to preserve a generation."

"Last year, this facility was looted." Michael opened his door but didn't get out.

"Is that why you are moving?" Mac asked.

"Yes." Michael sighed, "Until that moment, I never felt my life was in danger when working in country." His gaze looked distant, like he was back in that moment, seeing the violence unfold. "The camp was stormed by a group of armed men. We think it was M23 militants. They took all the supplies. Rachelle and I were held on the ground at gun point. I thought we were both goners."

Michael paused, locking eyes with Rachelle then continued. "They've been known to violently kill people and to burn everything to the ground. One of the guys put the barrel of his gun right up to my head. It was terrifying. The only reason I think they didn't shoot us was so that they could raid us again."

"They set us way back," Rachelle added. "The locals suffered the most. Who knows how many children died because we couldn't give them care for months. I wish we had a more permanent, safer facility."

"That *is* terrifying." Mac was shaken by the idea of how such violence was a very real threat to all of them. "Aren't you afraid they'll come back?"

Michael managed a sweet smile. "I can't say I'm not afraid. Hopefully they moved on and our next location is safer."

"Would you both like a tour?" Rachelle broke the somber moment.

"Sure, why not," Cameron answered without Mac's input. She didn't really want to stick around and had been looking forward to getting back to camp for a normal-ish day.

"Great!" Rachelle clapped her hands. "It's not often I get to show people what we do."

As they started toward the camp, a young woman in a volunteer uniform jogged up to meet them. She gave out a breathless hello before asking, "Are you Cameron?"

"Yes, that's me." Cameron stepped forward a bit.

"You have a message from a Chimp. I hope that isn't his real name. Anyway, he called our satellite phone."

"That man found our number?" Michael remarked. "Hell, it took me days to get it to pass on to my family back home."

"What did he say?" Cameron asked the woman.

She recited, "He needs you to get back to the ranch as soon as possible. He wants you to fly to Mombasa. The plane must leave within the next two hours."

"Did he say anything else?" Cameron asked.

"No, sorry."

Cameron looked at Rachelle, the corner of his eyes and mouth drawn down apologetically. "Maybe another time for the tour?"

"Maybe." Rachelle smiled, though her expression remained stiff, as if knowing if the tour didn't happen today, it would never happen.

"Take care." Rachelle hugged Mac. "You're doing great work."

The men clasped hands, wrapped one arm around the shoulder of the other, then gave a two-tap back slap, as man-hug etiquette deemed. "You guys keep saving those animals," Michael said to Cameron.

Then he hugged Mac.

"You too as well ... the people, I mean," Mac replied.

Rachelle walked up, then wrapped her arms around Cameron. He embraced her, pulling her into him and resting his chin on top of her head. She gently buried her face in the curve of his shoulder. Mac saw him whisper something into her ear. Nodding, Rachelle lifted her head as a tear rolled down her cheek. She playfully wiped it away on Cameron's shirt, giving him a coy look.

"Stay safe." Rachelle took a deep breath, then turned, half-trotting to the busy tents. Michael grabbed their bags from the Jeep and followed. Rachelle looked back once at Cameron. They gazed at each other until she turned around.

"Ready?" Cameron asked without looking away from Rachelle until she disappeared into a tent. Mac didn't answer ... he wouldn't hear her anyway.

As Cameron reversed out of the camp, Mac watched the faces of people lined up for help. Overwhelmed by the enormity of suffering, she was happy to leave it behind. But what Rachelle said about a more permanent place, gave her an idea.

I'll have to make a point to talk with Chimp later.

Chapter 20: I Insist

Mac lay on Texan ground, looking up into a starry night. She felt someone next to her.

Keene's voice, "You remember when we would go to that old drive in?" She turned and looked into his blue eyes ... or did they look coppery brown?

"Those speakers were awful." Mac ginned at the memory. "The movie was a James Bond film —"

"Goldfinger. 1964." He smiled and his features grew hazy to the point that she couldn't tell if his hair was brown or blond. "Isn't it a nice night?" Keene looked back at the stars.

Mac felt a pain deep in her heart. She rolled over to wrap her arm around Keene. Only she didn't feel him ... just a whisper of a memory of how it felt when their skin touched.

"He's not so bad."

"Who's not so bad?" Mac sat up and looked him. To Mac, he looked sad and tired.

"It's okay if you want to be with Cameron."

"Don't say that."

Mac felt a jolt. The ground began to shake. "Are we in an earthquake?"

He ignored her question. "It's okay if you want to be with him."

Another jolt rocked Mac. She looked to Keene in a panic ... he wasn't there. The starry sky began to blur.

"Don't go!" Mac reached out into nothing.

Another jolt jarred her, and something hit her head. At first, she believed it to be a rock, as her consciousness rose, she realized it was the Jeep's window.

"Sorry," Cameron apologized as he took in a sharp hiss of breath. "Did that hurt?"

"Huh? What the —"

"Another one coming." The Jeep bounced again, jerking them both forward and back. "Man, this road sucks. I was trying not to wake you."

"It's alright," Mac stated. But it wasn't. Nothing was alright. She rubbed her head to rid herself of the dream and the ache in her skull.

"Are we there yet?" she managed to mumble.

"Just pulling into camp now," Cameron exclaimed, seemingly oblivious to the fact she was annoyed with him.

He pulled up to the main office. Chimp was standing outside waiting for them. He walked down and met the Jeep at the steps before they could even get out of the Jeep.

"Cameron, I'm sorry I didn't mention this earlier, but there's so much going on. I need you to go to Mombasa and see Kendalie." Chimp glanced through the open window at Mac. "He will meet you at Fort Jesus tomorrow at noon."

"Why Mombasa? That's a long trek for a meeting. Couldn't I just call?"

"It's more than a meeting, Cameron. I feel he may have something you'll need to follow up on there. Take Mac. You will need her skills."

No, no, no, no, no. Mac's pulse raced. She wasn't mentally prepared to jump on a plane and head to Mombasa in the next hour. It wasn't about vanity; she hated to fly, and she wanted to check on the pregnant elephant.

Cameron started to protest, "I don't think—"

Chimp cut Cameron off with a wave of his hand. "This won't be dangerous, and Mac, your assistance is needed at one of the villages. There are farmers that are having issues with elephants eating their crops. There is help on the way, but if we don't follow up with an in person visit, they could get impatient and take matters into their own hands."

"I ... I need to take care of Fenny," Mac stuttered in protest. "And Amahle's baby will be coming soon."

"Fenny? Oh, the little fox I've heard of. Lebron will take care of Fenny and last report from Abebe said Amahle's not showing signs of labor."

"But—"

"And I'll cover your hotel and meal expenses," Chimp added. "Make a little mini vacation out of it." Chimp's words seemed more of an order than a request. And since Mac was a guest at the ranch, she felt obligated to go.

"Why aren't you going?" Mac asked, then seeing Chimp's pallor, already knew the answer.

"I'm not feeling well. The journey would be too much, and I would slow things down. We have a real chance to catch up with the poachers, and I don't want to waste it."

"You mean the Dragon?" Cameron raised his eyebrows.

Mac was excited at this news. To be able to shut the Dragon down would be a huge win for protecting elephants across Africa.

"If we're lucky." Chimp abruptly turned and walked away, signaling the conversation was over. He shouted behind him with a wave, "Kendalie will fill you in. The plane is at the airstrip, so get there as soon as you can. It's best to catch the daylight hours."

Dang it! I'm going to Mombasa whether I want to or not ... and I didn't get to run my idea by him. I guess it'll have to wait.

"Okay." Cameron turned to Mac, "Looks like we need to pack quickly." He put the Jeep into gear and started to back away before Mac could voice any additional concerns or protests.

Chapter 21: I Would Rather Walk

Mac felt like she'd been up all day and it wasn't even noon. After she and Cameron each packed a duffle bag, they headed to the grass landing strip that was located on the ranch. A sense of dread washed over Mac as a small plane came into view.

"Please tell me we're not flying in that!"

"Unless you want to drive for three days—" Cameron shrugged.

"Yes. Yes, I want to drive for three days. That plane's straight out of an *Indiana Jones* movie." Mac shifted uncomfortably. She knew there was no way out but up.

"Well, we don't have the time." Cameron shrugged. "Did you know, the plane in the movie was a Waco Aircraft Company UBF-2 with the registration OB-CPO that was an inside joke, a *Star Wars* reference. George Lucas always does clever stuff like that."

"It's times like these I'm reminded what a huge geek you are." Mac's mouth curved in a sarcastic smile.

"Anyway," he continued, seemingly unphased by her label, "this plane is quite a bit bigger than the one in the movie. It's a Cessna Caravan turboprop."

"Well, I was actually referring to the one in the *Temple of Doom*."

"Fair enough. At least this one is newer and has three landing wheels."

The Jeep rolled within a few feet of a small hut. Cameron got out and started towards the hut. He turned when he seemed to notice she wasn't following. He walked to her door and opened it. The sweet smell of oil and kerosene from the airplanes fuel filled Mac's nose.

"It took three Xanax to get me from Mombasa to the ranch. Oh my god! I forgot to pack it." Images of the plane crashing—on takeoff, while flying, and during landing—all ran through her head. She looked in the direction of her hut and the missing Xanax. "We need to go back."

"Calm down, Red." Cameron held out his hand and helped her out. "We don't have time for you to go back. Don't worry. It's perfectly safe, and if it crashes, you can tell me I was wrong."

Mac felt dizzy. Cameron gave her a concerned look.

"You look pale."

"You think I'm pale now? You should see me on a plane. I'm translucent."

A weathered gentleman stepped outside a modest hut. "Cameron!" the man exclaimed holding his arms out wide.

"Bruce! Good to see you again," Cameron called out. "It's been a little while." He waved then pointed at Mac. "This is Mac."

"Nice to meet-cha," the man spoke in an Australian accent. "I'm Bruce."

"Like the shark in *Nemo*?" Mac asked.

"No, like Bruce Wayne. My mother was a big *Batman* fan."

"Are you serious?" Mac responded.

"No, but I definitely had the name before the shark." He smiled, causing the crow's feet around his eyes to deepen. Mac followed Cameron reluctantly.

Mac, get a hold of yourself. This is perfectly safe, just look how old the man is flying it. He must have survived a few flights. Also, he looks familiar.

"Haven't I seen you before?" she asked.

"Last time I stopped at the ranch was a few months ago. Chimp's on my route when it comes to transporting gear and injured baby elephants to the mobile units."

"That's right. I was helping with the baby elephant, Qinisa. She was found alone and injured—missing part of her trunk. I hear she's doing well at the conservation park now."

"That's what I heard as well. Ya must have been really focused on the elephant to miss a handsome devil such as myself."

"Must have. You're most definitely unforgettable." Bruce smiled then looked perplexed when Cameron gave out a big laugh.

"Is that thing safe?" Mac gestured toward the plane.

"Safe as anything. The gas gauge is broken, but I think we have enough."

Mac looked at Cameron, with pleading eyes.

"He's kidding, Red. Relax." Cameron grabbed his backpack.

"I'm not kidding," Bruce said. "It's broken. Though, I did fill the tank, and she hasn't let me down yet. You can get up to nine hundred nautical miles from this baby."

"I would like to go back now." Mac turned and started to walk back to the Jeep.

Cameron put an arm around her and swung her round in a mini do-see-do. "It'll be fine," he said, as he nudged her in the plane's direction. "Plus, I'm going to need your help."

"So how much do you both weigh?" Bruce asked.

"You're kidding, right?" Mac looked back and forth between the men. "Right?"

"Well, I put you at one hundred and twenty-five," Bruce said. "This bloke, I'm thinking two-ten." Bruce held out his hands as if framing a movie shot.

Cameron chuckled. "I haven't weighed myself since the military, Bruce. That feels about accurate."

"Why are we worried about weight?" Mac slowed her pace.

"Just need to get my numbers, so I know how far we can fly." Bruce winked at Mac. "Don't worry, she should be able to just make it all the way there."

"Should?" Mac didn't know if he was kidding.

They reached the dirty white plane with a weathered red stripe running along its side. The door gave a metallic squeal as Cameron opened it. Inside smelled of dirt, animal, and worn leather. There were four seats and cargo space. It was the flying equivalent of a soccer mom van. Blankets and a wooden box of supplies were tied to the floor. Yellow cargo belts were off to the side. Mac had seen them used to secure baby elephants during flight.

"We need to get going." Cameron's voice was impatient.

Every nerve in Mac's body was telling her how stupid it was to get in the flying death box. Summoning her courage, she crawled in and put her seat belt on as tight as it would go. Her heart pounded in her ears.

"Good on ya." Bruce yelled back her as he climbed into his position in the pilot seat. "I checked everything out before ya got here, so we're ready to go." Cameron jumped into the front and buckled in.

"Why am I in the back?" Mac yelled as the propellers started to turn. It sounded as if she were in the middle of a large hair dryer.

"Well, if we do crash, you'll have better luck in the back." Bruce yelled back.

"Funny man," Mac stated.

Cameron turned and smiled at her. "You going to be all right back there, Red?"

"Yep. Just fine. Nothing to see here folks."

Inside, Mac wanted to scream and run from the plane. Instead, she sat back in what she hoped resembled a relaxed position.

Bruce started forward, then turned the plane and headed down a wide path of cut grass. The plane squeaked, jolted, and rattled as Bruce lined it up with the center.

"Hang on to your hats, lady and gentleman. Here we go." He pushed in the throttle. The plane quickly picked up speed.

Mac tightly held onto the seat as they rolled along the bumpy ground, her fingers aching as she dug them into the worn leather. Up ahead was a wall of grass. She envisioned the propeller blades mowing it down as they crashed through it. The plane went faster. The grass wall came closer. Mac put her hands over her face, moving one finger to the side so she could witness her demise.

There was the feeling of a little lift, then Bruce pulled back the yoke. The rattling and bumping dissipated into smoothness. Forces pulled her body up and her stomach down as the plane left the ground and seemed to just make it over the grass wall. A feeling of weightlessness was quickly replaced by an enduring push as the plane climbed. Pressed back into her seat, Mac dropped her hands, chanced a look to her left, and watched the ground getting further away.

Bruce called from the front, "Ya all right back there, lass?"

"Yep," was all Mac could manage to say. The plane rattled and jolted up and down unpredictably.

"Can't you fly around the bumps?" Mac complained.

"That's just the heat from the ground sending little pockets of air upward," Bruce replied. "I'll tell ya what. You point out the potholes, and I'll fly around them."

Cameron chuckled, yet Mac was not amused.

After a few more white-knuckled, stomach-dropping moments of dips and inclines, Bruce leveled the plane. He yelled over his shoulder, "Should be smooth from here on. Hey! Look over to your right."

Reluctantly, Mac leaned to her right and pressed her face to the window. They were flying over beautiful brown grassy terrain, sprinkled with trees. A curvy brown line of African forest buffalo came into view.

"There must be a hundred of them," Mac yelled. "Look! They're crossing a river."

The buffalo patiently waited their turn as two or three went in the water at a time. Not one paused, just followed the other blindly. Small calves struggled to keep up with their elders. It was an amazing conga line of horned reddish-brown beasts.

"That's so amazing," Mac yelled over the loud hum of the engine. Cameron was grinning at her. She smiled back.

Keene's voice echoed in her head, *he's not so bad*.

It was the phrase he'd said in her dream. She didn't want to think about that right now. She didn't know why, but she didn't feel right liking Cameron. Maybe she still mourned Keene, maybe she was afraid she might fall in love. And if she fell in love, it would kill her to lose someone again.

Chapter 22: I Just Want to Sleep

Light orange, pink, and blue colored a darkening sky as the sun set in Mombasa. Mac was relieved to see the small airport runway and its taxiways.

"Just in time." Bruce tapped one of the cockpit's dials. "We had a bit more headwind than I predicted." He smiled at Mac, then looked to Cameron ... who looked a little uneasy himself at that news. Mac tightened her seatbelt.

The aircraft's flaps lowered with a mechanical whirl, then the plane seemed to almost brake and drag through the air, losing altitude at a steady rate. The ground grew closer, and even though they were slowing, the plane seemed to be moving faster towards the runway at Moi International Airport. Mac reactively braced herself as the plane descended. They approached the strip from the land side. On the other side of the runway, in the dimming light, the usual dark blue and aqua waters of Port Reitz looked an ominous obsidian.

White buildings with pointed orange rooftops speckled the landscape. Green trees filled parks and lined streets and roundabouts. Mac focused on the amazing view of the city, avoiding images of crash landing into the water. She could clearly see the traces of the British who had colonized Mombasa and had imprinted their European culture throughout the town.

Mere feet above the black pavement, the aircraft seemed to hover in a suspenseful pause. Then gravity pulled the plane back down to the bosom of Earth. The wheels made a quick squeak as rubber gently kissed the tarmac before all three tires made firm contact. Mac welcomed the smooth and soft landing with a sigh of relief.

"Greased the landing," Cameron commented.

"Thanks, mate."

As Bruce taxied the plane into its parking space, Mac unbuckled her seat belt. When the plane stopped, she refrained from the cliché of jumping out and kissing the pavement.

"Chimp has a hotel for us," Cameron yelled as Bruce cut the engine.

Mac looked forward to sleeping in a real bed. "That was nice of him."

"Room and board come with the job, and he always sets me up at nice places when he can. Apparently, he really likes you because we're staying at the White Crown."

"One of the nicest ones here," Bruce added. "Lucky lady."

Mac sure didn't feel lucky. She felt apprehension and a sense that they were running out of time. Most of all, she felt tired.

"There should be a row of taxis out front. You shouldn't have any issues."

"Thanks." Cameron shook Bruce's hand before jumping out of the plane and opening the door for Mac.

Bruce turned toward Mac. "See, you didn't die."

"Not today, anyway." Mac disembarked from the plane and grabbed her luggage. "Are you going to be able to get the plane fixed before we head back?"

Bruce sniffed. "I will be sure to fix it right after I get a few beers and some shuteye. And be sure to take care of yourself, lass. Africa can be a dangerous place."

"Please. I'm a Texan. This ain't my first rodeo with a poacher." She tilted an invisible cowboy hat at Bruce.

***

The taxi pulled up to a beautiful white hotel. It was perfectly lighted to show off a decorative brown stone border, tall columns, and lush landscaping. Every corner had outdoor patios roofed with sea blue canvas arranged like conical tops of castle towers. Lancet windows adorned the second floor, adding to the romantic charm. It was the kind of hotel honeymooners would whisk off to after the formalities of a ceremony.

"I see where the hotel gets its White Crown name," Mac commented. "It's beautiful … too bad I didn't bring a swimsuit."

"That *is* too bad." Cameron winked. "If only we had more time."

The freshness of salt water and the slight unpleasantness of fish filled the air. Two bell hops quickly walked out and whisked their bags away. Cameron and Mac followed them into the lobby. Bright murals and art lined the walls in a rainbow of colors. Ornate mahogany chairs with red velvet cushions were stark against the dazzling white tile that led to the front desk.

"Wait here while I sort out the room."

"Room?" Mac asked.

"Don't worry. Two beds." Cameron smiled. "Chimp is generous but also frugal."

"Right. Frugal." Mac didn't really mind. She trusted Cameron, and she was so tired that she would sleep on a dirt floor with a dozen other people, if offered.

As beautiful as the hotel was, Mac barely remembered the walk to the room, but was pleasantly surprised when Cameron opened the door. Not only was the room something you'd see in a travel brochure, but a tray full of fruit, nuts, veggies, and breads were artfully displayed on a table. Along with bottles of water and a carafe of red wine.

"I'm beginning to love that man," Mac declared as she walked straight to the table. She sat and dove into the nuts and fruit. Her hunger overruling her sleepiness.

"I would hate to see you when you're really hungry." Cameron locked the door and claimed the bed closest to it by setting his bag on the mattress.

She mumbled through a mouthful of bread, "I'm just going to stuff my face, take a ten-minute shower, then go to bed."

Cameron held up his hands in surrender. He grabbed the wine and poured two glasses, then gave one to Mac.

"I don't know if this is the best food ever or if I'm just ravenous." Mac popped a slice of heart of palm into her mouth. She delighted at the crisp, crunchy, fresh taste.

"Little of both perhaps." Cameron sat down beside her.

"So tomorrow, what are we doing with this guy Kendalie?"

"He's going to hopefully give us some info on the poachers."

"And then what? We go after them? What about the elephants that need help in the village?" Mac guzzled her wine then filled her glass with water and drank it down. She didn't need a foggy head now or a hangover in the morning.

"We are just going to have to play this by ear." Cameron walked over to the balcony and opened the doors. A cool ocean breeze immediately filled the room, billowing the curtains like white waves.

Mac felt full and her eyes grew heavy, she picked up her bag and went into the bathroom. She was happy to have a real shower with hot water and turned the temperature as high as she could stand. The steam and heat relaxed her even more. If she weren't so tired, she would have stayed in the shower forever.

With wet hair, dressed in a T-shirt and shorts, she exited the bathroom. Cameron was shirtless at the table finishing up the food. He sat back, glass of wine in hand, and stared at her.

"Your turn." Mac tried not to look at his chest. It was defined and had just the right amount of curly blond chest hair to run fingers through.

He stood and passed by her so closely that her skin erupted in goose bumps. She admired his body and realized that he noticed her looking at him. *He must know he's hot.*

Not wanting to give him an additional ego boost, she quickly jumped into her bed and faced the window.

"The water pressure was awesome," she shouted at him. "Best shower I've had in months."

"I'm looking forward to it," Cameron responded in a silky low voice.

She heard his footfalls pause, as if waiting for her to look back at him. She didn't and the door creaked. Mac rolled onto the side she preferred to sleep on.

Cameron hadn't shut the door. From the bed, she could see the shower curtain. She closed her eyes to a sliver, allowing her to feign sleep, yet see the bathroom. Cameron turned the shower on, then disappeared.

The unmistakable sound of urine hitting the water made her uncomfortable, as if violating a privacy.

It obviously doesn't bother him, or he would have shut the door, she assumed.

The faucet squeaked and Mac could see his hands as he ran them under water, and the back of his head when he drank from the faucet and spit after brushing his teeth. Steam started to roll from the bathroom.

Cameron came into full view, dropped his pants, then his boxers, then stepped into the shower. His glutes were as perfect as the rest of him.

He either wants me to look or to join him. Why else would he leave the door open?

Mac could make out his naked form behind the white shower curtain. Human nature gave way to romantic ideations.

What would it be like to bathe him? And to be bathed by him?

Pleasant images ran through her mind. She let her mind wander. Before Cameron turned off the shower, she was asleep.

Chapter 23: Who Knew Jesus Had a Fort

The fragrance of saltwater and sand traveled on a warm gentle breeze through the hotel window. The room was quiet except for the sound of waves and distant squawks of gulls. Mac could feel herself being slowly dragged into her senses and out of her dark slumber.

She had managed to kick out from all the covers during the night. The artificial breeze from a bamboo ceiling fan cooled her skin. She peeked at the other bed. Cameron lay on his stomach, his muscular, tan back exposed, his waist down lay under a thin sheet.

Beep-beep ... beep-beep ... beep-beep.

Cameron shifted slightly and groaned. He reached blindly for his watch, looked at it, then groaned again as he sat up and leaned his back against the headboard.

"Morning," Mac mumbled. "I'm assuming that's our wake-up call."

He looked at her. She caught his eyes trail across her bare leg that poked out from the under the sheets. She didn't attempt to cover it. It was just a leg after all.

"Morning." He stretched his arms upward and yawned. "They should send up some food shortly. I ordered it last night. We can head out after we eat."

It was Mac's turn to yawn. She looked out the window. The green tops of palm trees were just visible out their window. Beyond that was sand and the blue of the Indian Ocean leading to a vast watery horizon.

She remembered when she and Cameron kissed the other day. There was an awkward flirtation between them now. An image of Keene came to mind, and she felt guilty again. She even grew a little angry at Cameron for causing her such inner struggles.

A light tapping came from the door.

"Room service," a male voice called quietly.

"I'm starved," Cameron exclaimed as he jumped up, dragging the sheet with him.

Mac wondered if he always slept commando or if he had been expecting something to happen between them last night. As he opened the door, she covered her exposed leg and sat up.

"Oh, wow." Mac was impressed as a hotel staff member, in a crisp white shirt and shorts, brought in a rolling cart topped with several silver-covered platters.

Cameron's eyes widened. "Did I order all that?"

"Courtesy of a Mr. Chimp." The man cleared the dishes from the night before, then set the table pouring two cups of coffee.

Steam and a nutty aroma rose from the cups.

"Miss?" the man looked at Mac. "I was told to inform you the muffins are vegan. Specially made for you."

"Thank you!" Mac was delighted.

He gave a quick nod. As Cameron reached for his wallet, the porter waved a hand, "No need, Sir. We were well taken care of." With a quick nod, he let himself out of the room.

"I need to travel with you more often," Cameron exclaimed. "I don't get this treatment from Chimp when I'm on my own."

"The coffee smells awesome." Mac jumped out of bed and rushed into a chair.

"Whoa!" Cameron laughed.

She pushed the eggs and bacon over to his plate, then quickly dove into the sliced tomato, papaya, and avocado, followed by a large bite of muffin with a coffee chaser.

"I've seen pythons chew their food more than you," Cameron commented.

"So, when do we head out?" she managed to mumble through bits of cinnamon and raisin muffin.

Cameron sat beside her, still wrapped in his sheet. The scene felt more like that of a couple on their honeymoon, than two people getting ready to take down a poaching ring.

"I'll call us a taxi after this." Cameron looked at his watch. "We both needed sleep, so I pushed the time as much as possible. It's almost ten now."

"Really?" Mac felt awesome. The sleep and the good food had done wonders.

Cameron stared at Mac.

"What?" Mac wiped at her mouth. "Is there something on my face."

"No, um … you just look pretty cute in the morning." Cameron shoved a huge bite of eggs in his mouth. The dripping yolk caused Mac's stomach to flip.

"I'd say the same to you, but you have chicken fluid on your chin."

Cameron made a show of licking it off.

"Gross." Mac scrunched up her face and stuck out her tongue, making him laugh.

The rest of breakfast was finished in a comfortable silence. Mac tried not to worry and to enjoy the perfect morning. She wanted just a few brief moments of not thinking about animals dying or life's struggles in general. The stresses of Africa and her job were starting to weigh on her. She missed her family.

"I'm going to spoil myself and take another shower," she declared. "Who know when I'll get another."

"You have about thirty minutes." Cameron informed her. "That should be plenty of time."

Mac picked up her bag and headed to the bathroom. "I showered two or three times a day in Texas. I'm just getting back to my clean-freak roots." Mac shut the door and enjoyed the luxury of indoor plumbing and hot water.

***

"I didn't think it was possible."

"What?" Cameron asked.

"That I could fear anything more than flying," Mac stated, her knuckles turning white while she gripped the door of the taxi as it took the roundabout at a quick clip. "I almost miss Bruce."

"I'm sure he'll be happy to hear that," Cameron answered, amused.

The taxi driver rushed through downtown Mombasa traffic with the grace of a bull. After several quick, jolting stops and starts, Mac hoped her wonderful breakfast would stay in her stomach.

The streets were littered with tuk-tuks in all the colors of a rainbow, bearing yellow plates with big brown writing. The traffic lanes were crowded and reminded Mac of the organized chaos of an ant hill. When the traffic slowed, people randomly crossed the street giving little concern for vehicles.

She watched as the driver sped past businesses and shops. Bikes came alongside the taxi with the cyclists paying no attention except on the road ahead.

The taxi drove by a brilliant white restaurant with an outside dining area covered by red tarps and enclosed by a railing. In front of the many shops, people gathered and sat on plastic chairs, talking.

A woman carrying a bald baby on her hip, too young and plain-clothed to tell if they were a boy or a girl, was standing on the corner waiting to cross. The baby looked at Mac as they drove by, probably taken with her unusual red hair. Mac smiled and waved. The baby's eyes remained fixated as a tiny fist waved back.

All the buildings seemed to be white and ocean blue. Many looked old and out of a 1950s movie. For the most part, the main street was clean. The driver drove beside the median, which was an oasis of walkways broken by evenly spaced oval islands of green grass and plants, a reminder that Mombasa was a tropical, coastal city.

Cameron leaned close to Mac's ear, "Kendalie will meet us in the ammunition store." He spoke loudly, to be heard over the driver's music.

"Ammunition store?"

"It's where they once stored ammo. Now, it's basically an empty space."

She was relieved as the driver rounded a corner and Fort Jesus came into full view. The fortress was made of thick yellow and black stained rocks. It had a fairy tale mystique of a castle rather than of a military stronghold.

The driver dropped them off at the entrance. A stone path lined with green trees led into the courtyard. Mac marveled at the history as they walked inside.

"It's just over here—" Cameron took Mac's hand and led her left. "By that gun platform," he pointed to a flat stone surface lined with cannons aimed out small holes in the stone wall.

"What, no sightseeing?"

"We can take the long way." He waved out his arm in a sweeping gesture and bowed, as if guiding her towards a ballroom floor. "This way, my Lady."

"Thank you, my Lord," Mac giggled as they walked up to the platform.

The view was perfect. The bright blue waters of the Indian Ocean lapped quietly against the beach. Mac could taste the salt in the breeze.

There were only a sparse number of people there; a small family, a group of young men who looked like they were making a social media video, and other small groups. If you stood still, you could hear everyone's conversation.

Cameron pointed at a diagram of the fortress. "See how it's shaped?"

"It looks like a person." Mac traced the outline with her finger. "Almost like a square gingerbread man with stumpy limbs. Was this for any military reason?"

"No. Maybe King Philip asked the architect, Giovanni Battista Cairati to make it in his image. Or maybe Giovanni just craved a gingerbread cookie." One corner of Cameron's mouth lifted in teasing grin. Mac reciprocated with a punch in his arm.

"Ow. Ha! Anyway, it's sixteenth-century Portuguese architecture, with a few changes made throughout the times. Omani Arabs and the British have also controlled it and made their own modifications."

"It's pretty impressive."

"It also functioned as a prison and as a lunatic asylum when the British colonized Kenya."

"You don't seem like the historian type to me," she stated matter-of-factly.

"History, no. But military history, I find that interesting." Cameron pointed to rows of what looked like iron-cast canons, some pointing through slits in the walls. "Take those cannons. The Portuguese cannons are the longer ones, and the British cannons are the shorter ones, yet the British cannons shot a hundred meters farther."

"The cannons are everywhere and pointed out in all directions," Mac observed.

"That's what's so great about the shape of this place. And down here—" Cameron took her by the hand again and led her down steps and through an entrance, "—is the armory."

"It looks more like a cave." Mac pulled her hand away. There was a chill as they entered below ground. The image of all the people who were jailed, insane, or died there, gave the structure a foreboding presence.

The room was quiet, and the corners were in almost complete darkness. It took a few minutes for her eyes to adjust.

A moving shadow caught Mac's attention. She jumped, and Cameron quickly placed himself between her and the shadow.

"Do we have a mutual friend?" the tall, slender man asked.

"Only if that friend is a Chimp," Cameron replied.

The man smiled broadly and held out his hand. "Kendalie."

"Cameron." He took Kendalie's hand and shook it. "This is Mac."

Kendalie's face softened as he took Mac's hand gently. "A pleasure."

Mac nodded and shook his hand. It was bony and cold. Her eyes adjusted to the darker room, and she was surprised to see a man that looked younger than Chimp. Kendalie had exotic features, high cheek bones, full lips, and unblemished, brown skin. If Kendalie and

Chimp were the same age, time had been more kind to Kendalie.

"I have news that ivory will be picked up from three villages and brought to the port tonight to leave for China," he said. "The shipment must be stopped before it departs."

"What time and where are the pickups?" Cameron asked.

"Exact times aren't known," Kendalie responded. "We missed the pickup at the first village. There were traces of where ivory may have been stored, but they beat us to the pickup. There are two more possible pickup sites just over five hours away. You'll be able to get to one just before nightfall if you leave soon. It's a small farming village that sits southwest of Kilawa, up the A109 then off the B7. There's a dirt road about eight kilometers past the village. Follow it until it forks and take the right one."

"Why not send the authorities?" Mac asked, wondering why such a task would be left to anyone who wasn't an official.

"I think there's a leak, which is why we're meeting in person. At this point, I don't know who I can trust. I haven't told anyone about the second village you will go to. I'll check the other."

"What are we supposed to do?" Mac asked. "We have no official capacity." *And, no way to legally stop and restrain poachers.*

Cameron added, "And how did you find out about the third village?"

"Through some less than honorable, but reliable sources," Kendalie replied. "Confirm if there's ivory. Keep them in sight if you can. Call me." He passed a card to Cameron. "I will contact the authorities."

Cameron put his hand on Mac's shoulder, "I would like to take Mac back to the hotel."

"There is another reason to go to that particular village. Crops are being raided by the elephants and the people have talked about taking matters into their own hands. I wanted to take this opportunity to diffuse the situation—Chimp said Mac would be helpful."

Mac felt the seriousness of the situation and wondered how she had gone from saving orphaned elephants to joining a poaching SWAT team. The situation was beyond her comfort level. Even so, she felt an obligation to help preserve animals. That is what Keene would have wanted.

"I have managed to contact the farmers and have opened discussions into using beehives to deter the elephants. It has been a slow process in moving the hives and the locals are getting restless. I need someone to go to the village, let them know that we are trying, and buy me two more weeks to get everything in place—that is where Mac comes in."

Gazing at Mac, Cameron asked, "Do you want to do this? You don't have to."

"Well, I had a massage and a pedicure booked for later today, but I guess I can cancel. Plus, I have to go if I can help people and elephants."

Cameron feigned a smiled. The slackness of his face told her he didn't like the situation.

"How are we getting there?" Mac looked at Cameron. "Not by taxi, I hope."

"I have a vehicle for you." Kendalie handed Cameron the keys. "It's the green one parked on the street out front. There is a cell phone in the glove compartment, but you will not always have signal."

A couple walked in the dark armory. Kendalie quickly changed the conversation to the lunch he was looking forward to eating. The couple looked uneasy as they walked around the small room. Mac couldn't blame them. The small space reminded her of a tomb. They left quickly.

Kendalie spoke, "There's one more thing—the man who leads the poachers, has a dinosaur tattoo."

Mac turned to Cameron, "The injured man in the hut mentioned a tattoo."

"Do you have a name?" Cameron asked.

"No. We do know he's an American with military training."

"That puts this on a whole different level." Cameron looked at Mac. "Are you sure you don't want to go back to the hotel? You don't have to go."

Mac nodded.

"Let's go stop some poachers, then!" Cameron declared.

Mac had more than a few doubts. She had dealt with poachers before, when she was back in Texas— and she had nearly died that first time.

Chapter 24: Road Trip

Tan dirt gave way to rust colored soil as Cameron turned onto the dirt road that led to the small farming village Kendalie spoke of. Mac shifted uncomfortably as her body ached from the nearly five-hour drive. They passed in front of a small community of huts made with grass and clay. Women sat outside weaving baskets and watching young children play.

"There's not much village," Mac stated.

"Hopefully. That makes our task easier."

Cameron slowed the car as they passed along a bumpy road lined with orange fruit trees. It didn't take long before they came upon a group of men tending to the crops.

Mac noticed Cameron focus on something or someone in the distance. When she looked, she didn't see anything.

"I'm going to look around," Cameron said turning the wheel to park, not moving his eyes from the spot.

"Alone?" Mac stared at him like he was crazy.

He gently put his hand on her knee. "We don't have a lot of time and I'm going to have to go see if I can find the ivory while you talk with them about their elephant problem."

Men were approaching the car.

"They have an elephant problem, and you know elephants."

"Sure, but—".

"It's just a couple dozen farmers who don't know what to do. You've been here long enough and know their challenges. Talk to them. I won't be far."

Not waiting for an answer, he opened the door and approached the men. Mac followed.

Okay, ... I can do this. Elephants' lives are depending on me.

"We were sent here to help with the elephants," he addressed one of the men. "Is there a leader or elder we can speak with?"

"I am Mobutu," said an older man with a weathered walking stick strode through the middle of the group.

"I am Cameron, and this is Mac. Kendalie sent us."

"Yes, yes. We have been waiting too long for his help." Mobutu tapped his stick impatiently on the ground, his deep brown eyes seeming to size up Cameron and Mac.

"He apologizes for the wait. These things take time, and he will have people out here in two weeks. He just asks that you hold on a little bit longer."

"Two weeks? We have already been waiting a month. It would be quicker to kill the elephant."

"No!" Mac shouted, surprising them both. She calmed herself then spoke patiently, "Please show me what is happening and maybe I can help until the beehives come."

Cameron looked at Mac with his chin down and eyebrows raised. She understood he was about to leave and was asking if she was good. She gave him a quick nod.

"I am going to look around the area, please show Mac your troubled areas, she is an expert in her field and can help."

The old man waved his walking stick in the direction of their crops. Mac followed Mobutu, while Cameron headed in the direction of the huts.

I have a bad feeling about this.

Chapter 25: Unwelcomed Guests

Gacoki stood at the side of a hut. He watched as a green car rolled past him. *This could be a problem,* he thought. So far, the job to pick up ivory had been easy. *The unexpected visitors could complicate things.*

"If we move fast, we could be out of here before they find us," he said to the American, Jacob.

Jacob stood against a tree with his brown cap pulled low on his forehead. He had also noticed the company. "Let's get started then."

"Where's the ivory?" Gacoki whispered.

"Behind here." Jacob gestured for him to follow.

Gacoki looked quickly back over his shoulder. The car was stopped now. There was a woman and a man. He saw the man look in their direction and he quickly moved around the hut.

"Do you think they are with the authorities?"

"Nah," Jacob answered as he tapped lightly on the hut's door. "They don't look official."

A middle-aged man opened the door. He had one eye that was the color of milk, and the other eye was brown, dull, and on its way to blindness. He seemed to contemplate them for a moment. Gacoki had an unsettling feeling, as if the white eye could see the black in his heart.

"Follow me," the man finally said.

They walked around back to another small wooden structure. A piece of faded red cloth hung as a door. Jacob went through first. Gacoki looked quickly around to ensure they hadn't been followed then went inside.

"Holy mother of ... how long have you kept this here?" Jacob asked.

"There must be at least forty tusks here." Gacoki's eyes went wide at the sight. This village was their last stop before the port, and though the other stops had large piles of ivory, this load was the biggest yet.

"We have collected it for many months," the man replied. "We expect to get paid fairly."

"Hiding it in plain sight," Jacob stated, putting his hands on his hips. "Clever."

"Or stupid," Gacoki added.

Jacob turned to Gacoki. "We need to get this out of here, fast. Before those visitors come around."

"Yes. I'll get the truck," he told Jacob. "Am I to bring this to the Golden Dragon?" Jacob's head cocked at his statement.

"You think he's going to meet us on the dock, shake our hands, and say attaboy?"

The American's was smug and cocky. Gacoki didn't like his attitude.

"What's it to you if you meet him or not?" Jacob continued. "Trying to get my job?"

Jacob moved closer to Gacoki, but Gacoki stood his ground. Jacob had a good foot over him, and Gacoki refused to blink in the withering gaze of Jacob's cold blue eyes. His grandmother always said: 'those with blue eyes are possessed by the devil'. She may have been right.

"I will not be taken advantage of," Gacoki told Jacob. Jacob surprised him by laughing and giving him a heavy pat on the back.

"I misjudged you, Gacoki. You got guts. You may be worth keeping around."

Gacoki took the American's show of affection as a good sign. Such trust would only help him.

Jacob pointed to the truck, "Go get her started while I pay this man. You get this done, and I'm sure you'll move up."

That was all Gacoki wanted to hear. The quicker he moved up, the quicker he would meet the Golden Dragon, and the quicker he would kill him.

Chapter 26: Old Friends United

The light was almost gone, which gave Cameron some cover. He moved smoothly through the small village, hiding at the sides of the scattered huts. Earlier, he saw a man in a cap watching him and Mac when they got out of the car. He headed in that direction. After slipping around a hut, he took a knee, then peeked around the corner.

There was a truck pulled up to what resembled a small storage structure. Cameron felt guilty for leaving Mac alone. *She's smart and should be able to reason with them.* Plus, they had a mission ... to stop the move of the ivory. And the mission came first.

A black man came out of the hut carrying a long package wrapped in cloth then placed it into the back of the truck. Another man, who looked like he lived in the village, stood beside the hut entry.

Where is the man in the cap?

A *click* came from behind him. Cold steel dug into his head.

"Officer Stephenson, what an honor to see you again."

"I'd know that sarcastic voice anywhere. Hello, Gunny." He slowly raised his hands in surrender. "Long time no see, old pal."

Images of Gunnery Sergeant Jacob Perry flashed through his memory, and Cameron couldn't tell if this meeting was a good or a bad thing. He didn't think Gunny Perry would kill him. He also would never have pictured him standing behind him with a gun at his head. *This day is full of surprises.*

"I think we should be on a first name basis, don't you? After all, we're no longer in the Marines, and we seem to be in an intimate situation ... to which I have the advantage." As if to emphasize his point, Gunny Perry slightly pushed Cameron's head with the gun.

"Ow! Okay, Jacob," Cameron replied. "Nice to see you again. Wish it was under better circumstances."

The pressure of the gun decreased and then disappeared.

"Turn around slowly," Jacob instructed. "Don't try anything and don't get up."

Cameron slowly turned to face his old acquaintance. He glanced quickly at Jacob's arm. A red velociraptor's orange eye stared at him. The dinosaur covered what used to be an American flag tattoo. Remnants of some stars and stripes were faintly visible underneath the reptile's muzzle. Anger filled Cameron. "Still making poor choices, I see."

"Like it?" He tipped his arm slightly. "They did a good job, don't you think?"

"Why would you—"

"Because the US government screwed me. I wasn't going to permanently wear something that reminded me of how my *pals* turned their backs on me."

"I remember now. You pissed off the wrong person and they "other than honorably" discharged you."

"Yeah, and that limited my benefits. I have PTSD ... they were supposed to help me."

"Dude, it was a bum deal. I agree. But is holding me at gun point necessary? I mean, I didn't have anything to do with that."

Jacob's eyes stayed locked on Cameron's. "I have no beef with you Capta—Cameron. At least I don't have one yet."

"Why are you doing this?"

"Don't pretend you're all high-and-mighty. I know about you. You act like you're all into saving wildlife. You're a hired gun, just like me. You just chose to be on the side that doesn't pay as much."

The truth in Jacob's words hurt. "I admit the money is what got me here, but I see a bigger purpose now."

"A bigger purpose?" Jacob's face screwed up into a grimace. "Do you think you will save them? It's only a matter of time until they're all gone."

Cameron kept looking for a moment to act on, only Jacob's gun never wavered. Jacob was well trained; Cameron should know because he had trained him. *I hope Mac is having better luck than me.*

Chapter 27: Can't an Elephant Get a Snack?

The old man led Mac to the edge of the village where he pointed his weathered walking stick at a small field of corn. Thick, muddy paths of broken and flattened stalks were scattered throughout the field. Orange trees stood on the outer edges, their branches broken and stripped of fruit.

"*Tembo*," Mobutu stated simply then, "elephant." He gestured to a stretch of forest.

"The elephants come from there?" Mac asked. The old man nodded.

The villagers viewed the elephants as destructive, dangerous, giant pests. The elephants probably felt the same way about them. She knew elephants tended to leave protected areas when crops, especially those with sugar, began to ripen. Oranges would be a huge temptation for hungry elephants trying to survive in a shrinking habitat. However, the people were also trying to survive. Mac had to find a middle ground and negotiate for the elephants.

Looking around, she noticed old tires, boxes, and wires littering the area.

"We must kill them, before they eat all of our food," a man called from behind her. She turned to see a small group had followed them. "The elephant, or elephants, could return tonight."

Noise. We need something to deter them. Her eyes traveled back to the trash. *Yes, that will do.*

Mac turned to face the men. As the sun sunk lower into the horizon, they seemed to be getting more anxious, in preparation for the elephants that may show up. Her heart thumped in her chest as she built the nerve up to speak.

"My friend, Kendalie, is working with a charity to bring you bees." She was encouraged to see all eyes were on her and they were quiet. "The elephants come here because they are hungry."

Grumbles and curses responded.

"Please, hear me," Mac raised her voice. "They are hungry, like you. They have families, like you. They are losing their land, just like you. They can learn not to come here." She had their full attention now. "The solution *is* the bees. The elephants fear bees and will not pass the hives if they hear bees buzzing." She continued, "You can also bring money into the village by selling honey to hotels and tourist shops."

"So, we are to wait months until bees come? Our families will starve by then," yelled someone in the crowd.

"The bees will arrive in two weeks. I promise. I can help you in the meantime. You have an alarm system right here." Mac pointed to the trash. "You have the equipment now to start protecting your village. The old boxes, metal, and tires can be hung on a wire. The elephants will be wary of the hanging objects and the metal will create noise when the elephants try to cross. This will deter them."

Discussions in the group followed. She felt this was an encouraging sign they were talking, and that gave her hope.

"I'll show you. Please gather some wire, boxes, and metal."

Mobutu nodded to the men, and they scattered to find the material. She knew what she said and did now could mean the difference between the life or death for these elephants— she hoped her idea would work.

The men brought long wire and she helped them pick a spot to hang it. Then, they strung up a large tire, scrap metal, and a box at shoulder height.

"Do this as much as you can around the crops." She jiggled the wire. Loud metal *clanging* and *clanking* traveled down the hanging objects. "I will ensure you get the bees and anything else needed to deter the elephants," Mac promised, hoping Kendalie would follow through.

Mobutu seemed pleased with the elephant barrier and thanked her.

"Have you seen anyone else here today? Someone not from the village?" She turned slowly in a circle, looking for Cameron.

"Yes, two men with a truck."

"When was this?" she asked.

"Not long before you arrived." He pointed in the same direction that Cameron had headed earlier— and he wasn't back yet.

This isn't good.

"Thank you … and I will ensure the bees arrive." Mac could only hope the village would keep their word and Kendalie would be able to keep his. She jogged in the direction Mobuto pointed.

Chapter 28: Three's a Crowd

Cameron was at eye level with the barrel of Jacob's Glock 9mm. A pebble dug into his knee, and he could feel blood soak his pants. Cameron discretely scanned the ground for something to use as a weapon.

"I will admit," Cameron confessed, "that I didn't come to Africa too concerned about elephant welfare in the beginning. But I've changed." He spied a couple of large rocks.

"Don't even think about it," Jacob stated, sounding bored. "I don't plan on shooting you, but don't make me change my mind. If the choice is between you or jail, let's just say I'm not going to jail."

"I can't let you leave with the tusks."

"Who said I'm here for tusks? I'm just picking up supplies." Jacob smiled.

"Give me a break. You're—"

"I'm getting supplies, and you and your girlfriend are going to go back to your little ranch and live happily ever after saving elephants," he chuckled. "Well ... some of them."

Cameron felt a pang in the pit of his stomach when Jacob mentioned Mac. He had put her in danger. *She's far away with the villagers, so she should be safe*, he told himself.

A flash of red hair appeared from behind one of the huts in the distance. *Are you kidding me?*

He quickly moved his eyes back to Jacob. *Please let her stay where she is and not do anything stupid,* he pleaded to God. Footsteps scraped the dirt behind him. A sharp pain shot through his body as a strong force sent him face-first into the ground.

"What the hell did you kick him for?" Jacob shouted. "I have things under control."

"I finished loading all the tusks," said a black man. "I'm dripping in my own sweat and smelling of rotten meat, while you're having a conversation with this man. I heard your babble. You know this American?"

"Yeah, so?" Jacob countered.

"You're wasting time with your talking." The man gestured at Cameron. "We can't play your games, American. It's time to go. If he and that woman are here, more may be on the way."

Cameron rose to his knees and clenched his fists.

"Put your hands behind your back," the man demanded.

"Chill. I'll cooperate, but you kick me like that again, and I'll break your leg."

Jacob chortled, "He'll do it too. Only then I'd have to shoot him. We don't want that, do we?"

Unwilling to turn this standoff into a fight or a situation in which Mac might get hurt, Cameron placed his hands behind his back. He didn't see any way out that didn't get him killed. He would have to do what he was told. If Jacob wanted to kill him, he would.

A rough material entwined his hands.

"Hey, ease up man," Cameron hissed. "I'd like to keep my hands." He licked his lips, then spit out mud, tasting earth. A rock had scratched his face and it burned as sweat ran across the cut.

"Stand up," the man directed.

Cameron rose to his feet; the world went dark and smelled of burlap.

"A sack over my head? Is this *really* necessary? It's not like I haven't seen you already." He felt a string tighten around his neck and his heart began to race, as panic started.

He had been claustrophobic since he was a child. When he and his best friend, Andy, took turns rolling each other up in blankets like a burrito. Andy had the theory it would be hilarious to not let him out. But the blanket was so big that it cut out all the light and Cameron felt he couldn't breathe. He screamed and cried for several minutes, though his friend later told his parents through tears and running snot, it was only seconds.

He had no idea how long it really was because he had passed out in the blanket and had woken to his mother shaking him. His mom had held him tight and cried—she had believed him dead. His friend got a whipping from his dad that had been so bad he didn't talk to Cameron for a week. He didn't care. Andy deserved it.

Ever since the "burrito incident," Cameron had passed out a couple of times from panic attacks. One happened as a teenager while in a haunted house when he had to crawl through a confined space to get to the next room, and another happened when Marine buddies talked him into spelunking in Utah. He hadn't gone very far into the cave before he started to get dizzy. To save face, he had lied and told them his guts were bad and he might have food poisoning.

And now, he was close to passing out again. He was pushed forward and became disoriented. As he stumbled, he managed to choke out, "I can't breathe."

"If you can talk, you can breathe." The man shoved him again.

"Hey! Ease up there, Rambo." Jacob held out his hands palm facing out. "He's not going anywhere."

Don't pass out. The pressure of the tie around his neck constricted Cameron's breathing. *Don't ... pass ... out*, he told himself again. The stench of death and rotted meat from the bag filled his nose.

Cameron started to retch.

A boot to his back pushed him down to the ground.

"That's enough!" ordered Jacob.

After a *thunk* and a grunt, something fell to the ground near Cameron. His neck muscles tensed as he started to gag, making the tie around his neck feel even tighter.

The world started to spin. The blood in his legs felt like it was turning into ice, crystalizing his blood as it started to travel up his body. He wasn't winning his fight for consciousness. Some part of him was aware of yelling, then the sound of a truck, before everything began to fade.

Instantly, he saw dim light and smelled fresh air as the sack was pulled off his head. He looked up at the face of an angel with fire for hair.

"Oh my God! Are you okay?" the angel asked.

Then blackness consumed him as he passed out for the fourth time in his life.

Chapter 29: Humble Pie

The sun had just set, leaving barely enough light to see. The villagers had quieted. Mac held Cameron's sweaty head in her hands. He lay limp but breathing.

"Cameron." She gently shook him. When he didn't respond, she rolled him to his side, untied his hands, then rolled him onto his back again. She remembered from first aid training that most fainting spells lasted only seconds and that she needed to raise his head and place something under his knees. Nothing was handy for his knees, but she propped his head on her lap.

His face was hot, sweaty, and slack. With the tenderness of a mother nursing a sick child with a fever, she brushed pebbles and dirt away from his eyes, then softly traced her finger across his forehead, wiping his wet hair to one side.

Cameron's eyes fluttered open. He looked around wildly. Mac gently rested her hand on his cheek.

"Red?"

"It's okay," Mac said softly. "You passed out." His body tightened and he tried to get up. "Whoa, no, you're not going anywhere for at least ten minutes."

"Where's … Jacob?" He clumsily tried to get up again and Mac easily pulled him back down onto her lap.

"They are both gone. Just wait a few minutes. Besides, we know where they're headed. I'll call Kendalie when we get back to the car."

"Um, okay." Cameron rested his head against her and hissed as he rubbed his wrists. In the dim light, Mac could just make out the red burns the twine had made.

"You must not have had a lot of air with that nasty bag over your head."

"Did I pass out for long?" Cameron groaned and shifted his position. He looked up at her from her lap.

"You came to quickly, after I got the bag off." He sat up and spit.

"Gross," Mac remarked.

"I can still taste the rot and the dirt of the bag." Cameron wrinkled his nose and spit again. "What was in that bag?"

"Better you don't know."

Cameron looked at her for a moment, as if assessing her. "You keep surprising me."

"What do you mean?"

"You're not what I expected, not like my first impression of you. You're a lot stronger."

They sat in silence for a moment before Cameron sniffed and wiped his mouth with the back of his hand. "That man back there, the big guy with the tattoo, he's an old—I wouldn't say buddy—we knew each other from the military. His name is Jacob Perry. He was a Gunnery Sargent when I knew him."

"Wow, it really is a small world." Mac considered the odds. "Did Rachelle know him too?"

"No. Different assignment."

"Does this change things?"

"It shouldn't." Cameron sat up and faced her.

"Doesn't it?" She pressed him. "Because friends shouldn't let friends get tied up."

"He wasn't a bad guy, the guy I knew. Marines are brothers forever." He stood up slowly. "He could have killed me but didn't."

Mac looked up at Cameron, who seemed to be steady on his feet. When he held out a hand and helped her up, she knew he was back to his alpha-dog self. The experience was the first time Mac had seen Cameron helpless and human.

"Cameron, he's breaking the law."

"He's a brother-in-arms."

Silence stood between them for several seconds.

I wonder how many elephants Jacob has murdered or had a hand in murdering.

Mac could feel a divide in the way they viewed life. Even though they had a passion to care for and protect wildlife, she realized they had vastly different ideals. She wanted to like him … knew they were both attracted to each other … but deep in her gut knew it would never work. *Just like how his relationship with Rachelle didn't work.*

All that didn't matter now.

"Brother-in-arms or not, we have to stop him."

Cameron didn't disagree.

Chapter 30: Tired of Playing

"Explain to me again how we are going to get in," Gacoki snapped at Jacob as he drove slowly on the bumpy road with his lights.

Even with his lights off, he had no trouble seeing. The ambient light from the harbor was bright enough to see the rocks on the dirt road. Gacoki was tired of this mission and was ready to be done with it.

Jacob pointed. "There, see the light poles? See the one where the light is out? Drive in that direction."

"I see nothing," Gacoki argued. "Even so, there's the matter of the fence."

"Wait for it." Jacob held up his hand. "There." He pointed to the side of the road.

At first, only the fence was visible. As they drew closer, he understood the illusion. There was a part in the fence line with a light out, and it had a gate. The gate was propped open.

"Stop at the gate. I need to drop something off."

Gacoki drove through the gate then stopped.

Jacob took a small box from the back and set it behind a bush near the gate. He jumped back in the truck, looked at Gacoki, and shrugged. "My inside man likes his Cuban cigars and a little bit of coke."

This poaching ring is bigger than I assumed. Gacoki shook his head then drove on. They seemed to have people everywhere. Would killing the head of the snake be enough? Or would another snake take its place?

"Just go straight," Jacob said, tilting his chin in the direction. "When you get to the road closest to the pier, turn right. Then keep going until you reach ships."

They drove down to the pier. Three big ships with cranes loading cargo boxes, came into view.

Jacob tapped Gacoki on his arm. "It's that way," he said while pointing right. "Toward the black and red ship."

Gacoki felt anticipation rise though him. *I will finally come face-to-face with the Dragon. I will be able to kill him, then go back to an honest life. The debt of my father's death will be settled.* He had yet to decide if he would kill Jacob because he almost liked the American.

He parked close to the black ship and three open containers. The ship bore a red stripe with white Chinese symbols and below it the words *Floating Orchid* in English.

"Now what?"

"Now, we should see—" Jacob looked around then pointed to two men. "Them. One is the supervisor, and the other is a port inspector who accepts bribes." Jacob smiled broadly. "See those two containers?" He pointed again. "Those are the modified containers. Once we get the ivory loaded, they'll put timber in and move the containers to the ship."

Jacob waved at the men, and one of them gave him a tip of his hat.

"That's the sign." Jacob clapped his hands then rubbed them together. "Back up to that blue container with the open doors. Get as close as you can. I'll even help you unload this time."

Gacoki backed the truck up to the first container. Neither the supervisor nor the port inspector came over. Both he and Jacob got out of the truck. By the time Gacoki got to the rear of the truck, Jacob was already dismantling the back wall of the first container.

"You can start laying them down in here while I get these other panels off, then I'll help you."

"Where are the other men?" Gacoki frowned. "This was supposed to be a drop and run." He wondered if six thousand had been enough to ask for delivery and unloading.

"I pay them to look away, not to assist. They don't know what we have, nor do they want to. Now hurry. If my pal back in that village decides he didn't like to be beaten and tied up, he'll be here soon. You know, I always pictured him as the bondage type. Most of the quiet ones like the kinky stuff."

"Kinky stuff?"

"Never mind, just come on. We have about thirty minutes."

While Jacob removed the panels to the hidden storage, Gacoki unloaded and carefully place the tusks into the container, which was lined with a thin protective foam.

"What happens after thirty minutes?" Gacoki huffed as he strategically placed a large tusk into the container.

"These containers will be picked up with or without us in them. Best we be gone by then."

The idea of being stuck in a container made Gacoki shudder. He picked up his pace as Jacob moved on to the next container to remove more panels.

Chapter 31: On the Road Again

It was almost midnight when the lights of the car illuminated a sign stating Kilindini Harbour was the next exit. Mac scanned the road ahead for the exit marker. Cameron had wanted to drive; however, Mac insisted that someone who had just passed out wasn't the best choice as driver. Resigned to her resolve, Cameron had settled for copilot and the task of waiting for cell tower connection so he could call Kendalie. He had been unable to contact him until now.

"Kendalie, finally. I—" Cameron listened intently before saying, "Sounds like your suspicions were true. We were kind of luckier. The cargo should be at the port now. We just got here … yes … yes, send them right away." He paused again before saying, "Track, but don't engage. Got it." Cameron hung up.

"We were luckier? Is that what you call what we went through?" Mac was upset at the lack of detail Cameron had given to Kendalie. "No mention of Jacob, no mention of passing out."

"We can all talk about it over a beer later. For right now, what he needs to know is that we didn't recover the ivory, that we know it was there, and that it's now at the harbor. This is a mission, Mac. Long conversations about feelings and relationships don't matter right now."

"Excuse me?" Mac felt flush with anger. "You think that's what I'm talking about? Hell, no. I'm talking about how you have a direct relationship with one of the poachers." She took one hand off the wheel to point at herself. "I may not be military. And I may not understand the protocol for mission communications. But I do know when someone is purposely withholding information." Mac glared at the road because she didn't know what she would do if she looked at Cameron.

"I'm sorry. That was wrong of me to say. I'm just on edge."

Silence conveyed Mac's refusal to accept his apology.

"Kendalie told me he was on his way back from his team's raid," Cameron said. "It was a false lead."

Mac continued to listen, staring at the road, avoiding looking at his face, as she took the exit.

"He said he would send police to the harbor."

"If there's a spy in the group," Mac responded tersely, "how do we know they won't tip off the Dragon?"

"Kendalie is contacting a hand-picked crew, which may take a little longer."

"What are we going to do when we get there? Watch them load the cargo and leave?"

"There is no we. *I* am going to make sure they get caught, and *you* are going to stay in the car."

"Because you did such a good job last time," she hissed through pursed lips, tightening her grip on the steering wheel.

Cameron flinched at the verbal blow. "*Because* of last time. They had guns. You don't need to be involved in that."

The lights of the harbor came into view. A city of iron cranes poked out the top of the landscape like tall buildings. She turned on her blinker and followed the signs toward the entrance gates.

"Look, Mac, I really am sorry. I'm not used to doing things with a civilian partner, and I don't know what's going to happen." Cameron placed his hand just above her knee and squeezed slightly. "I don't want to see you hurt. Promise me you'll stay safe." The pressure on her leg didn't soften. It wasn't unpleasant, and it kept her attention.

"Sure," she stated flatly, taking time to look in his eyes.

He seemed satisfied, released her knee, then sat back. She missed his hand on her knee, yet she also wanted to punch him in the throat.

The entrance was under several bright lights. The path blocked with traffic arms.

"How are we going to get clearance in?" she asked as she pulled up to a gate guard.

"I got it." Cameron leaned over her as she rolled down the window.

"Hey, Samuel." Cameron gave a two-finger salute. "We're in a hurry."

"Go on in. We just got the call, and the authorities are on the way. We told them to not turn on their sirens; we will see if they listen."

"Thanks, my man. Any idea where to?"

"There are three ships at the portside freight terminals." He pointed in the general direction of the docks.

"Drive that way." Cameron pointed for Mac to go right.

The guard nodded at them, then the traffic arms went up. Mac accelerated through the entry then followed the road.

Although it was nighttime, the bright lights turned the harbor into daytime. Warehouses and office buildings were on their left, and a maze of multicolored steel containers lined the road. She assumed they were waiting to be loaded onto boats or to be picked up and taken to their destination.

"Over there!" Cameron pointed in the direction of three huge ships. "That one on the left, the grey one, looks like it's getting ready to go."

"There are three boats. How do you know which one?"

"The first one is about to depart. We can park in the middle though."

"We left about thirty minutes after they did," Mac stated as she turned down the path Cameron had indicated. "They may still be loading."

"This is good." Cameron pointed to a big space between a stack of containers and a metal building. Mac pulled in and cut the engine and lights.

"Wait here." Cameron got out.

"I could check out another ship," she reasoned.

Cameron turned. "The best and safest thing you can do right now is to wait here. I may need you, and I won't have time to go looking for you or to worry about you." Cameron turned and ran into the maze of containers.

Slouched in the driver's seat, her arms crossed, Mac watched a crane swing a big blue cargo box over the car and in the opposite direction Cameron traveled. It looked to be headed toward a black and red ship. She reminded herself that they loaded ships all the time, so that one container didn't mean it was the one with the ivory.

I should at least let him know. She went to open the door then stopped, remembering his "order" to stay put. She hit the steering wheel in frustration. They didn't have much time and they may have already lost the poachers. *Just stay in the car*, she told herself. *That is what you are supposed to do. Of course, there wouldn't be any harm if I just take a peek at the ship. Look for Jacob or that other guy, then return. That should be okay.*

Mac watched the cargo box lower onto the ship's deck.

I also promised the herd I'd keep them safe. If we don't take the poachers down now, my herd could be next, and I'm not letting anyone mess with Amahle's baby. Besides, I'm not going to get close.

Without another thought, she was out the door.

Chapter 32: Oh, Where Has My Poacher Gone?

Forklifts ran back and forth in a choreographed industrial ballet as Cameron jogged between the maze of colorful containers. He ducked as a shadow flew over him like a large prehistoric bird. It was a cargo box. Cameron watched as the crane operator guided it to the black ship then slowly lowered it into the ship's belly.

There are hundreds of containers here. Where is Jacob or his friend that put the sack over my head? If I find that guy, I owe him a punch in the face.

A loud *hoot* filled the night.

Dammit, a boat is about to leave the dock, which means time is running out. How am I going to find Jacob in this mess?

Cameron ran down the pier, looking between the container for any signs of the men or the ivory. When he caught a glimpse of something, he stopped and backed up. It was the truck they had saw in the village.

Cautiously, he approached it. There was no movement. He looked in the cab. There were worn leather seats and empty soda cans. *Nothing to see here.* Around the back, he pushed a green tarp aside. It was empty.

"You, mate," A large, burly man called out to him with an Australian accent, jogging towards him. He was wearing a yellow jacket with reflective patches and a hard hat. Cameron assumed he worked on one of the ships.

"You have any business here? This isn't a place for tourists," he said breathlessly.

"I'm not a tourist," Cameron answered flatly. "I'm looking for the drivers of this truck. They're involved in an illegal transport of ivory."

The man raised his eyebrows. "The next boat leaving is the one headed for China, back that way." He pointed in the direction Cameron had come from. "It's a large black and red cargo ship. I remember seeing it on the schedule. My vessel goes out after them."

"Are you kidding me?" He pointed to the black ship. "I take it yours is the black one."

"That's the one. The *Atlantic Express*." As if to confirm the Aussie's statement, a boat sounded another long wailing noise. The sound came from behind him.

"Looks like you may be too late, mate."

Cameron wasn't sure if the guy was lying. Australia still had legal domestic markets for buying and selling ivory, and the tusks could be on his boat. But he was dealing with the Dragon. His money was on the boat heading toward Asian markets.

"Not yet, I'm not. Thanks." Cameron took off at a full run. Due to his survival training, he had no trouble recognizing the way he had come. The car soon came into view.

Mac wasn't there. He flung open the doors, hoping that she was asleep in the back.

"Dammit, Mac!"

The ivory quickly took a back seat as his concerns focused on Mac. He knew where she went and sprinted in the direction of the red and black ship.

Chapter 33: What Dragon?

The last container had been lifted onto the ship, and everyone seemed anxious to see it leave port. Chen, Bai, and Jiang had arrived to confirm the cargo's delivery right before the containers were lifted. Sweat dripped into Gacoki's eyes while he watched Jacob speak with Chen.

Look at them. All the money they will get and what do men like me ever get? We are the ones in danger. My father died doing this, to put food on our table, while people like them wear suits and drive around in fancy cars, eating and drinking till they are full. Gacoki could feel anger rising.

Jacob and Chen laughed about something. All the niceties and stalling wore Gacoki's patience.

"What is this?" he asked. "Where's the Dragon, Chen?"

All four men turned toward Gacoki. Jiang and Bai looked at him, as if addressing Chen by his first name directly was stepping out of place. Gacoki noticed Jiang had his hand on the butt of a gun as they both started to move. Chen barely lifted his hands, and they stood down like well-trained dogs.

"Do you really think the Dragon would come in person?" Chen sneered. "Why are you so interested in meeting him? You'll get paid. Or is the money from my hands not good enough for you?"

Knowing it was best to not let his past pain, struggles, and anger get the best of him, Gacoki controlled his tone. "I want to meet the man I'm working for. How can you give loyalty to a ghost?"

"You work for me." Chen's smile had disappeared. "Jacob tells me you interfered with an American."

Gacoki pointed at Jacob, "He was talking with that man. We were wasting time."

Chen's head snapped quickly to look at Jacob. His eyes flared with a look of distrust.

"He's an old military associate," Jacob shrugged. "He won't be a problem. Killing him would bring too much attention, and the authorities, to us. If he comes again, I'll take care of him."

Seeming to calm, Chen responded, "See that he doesn't become an issue." He barely looked over his shoulder to his men. "Bai, get the car. I'm satisfied with the cargo, so pay the man, Jacob."

Jacob handed Gacoki a roll of bills.

"This should make you feel better, my little African friend."

By the size of the roll, it looked to be all of what he was owed. Gacoki snatched the cash from his hands. Unfortunately, he would have to wait for another day to kill the Dragon. "This will help." He walked in the direction of the truck.

"What about her?" Jiang growled; his words were barely audible. "A friend of yours as well, Jacob?"

A flash of red disappeared behind a large container. Gacoki had no trouble remembering her.

"That is the same woman from the village. She was with the *mpumbavu* American."

"Hey, watch the *stupid American* cracks," Jacob snapped. Gacoki didn't like the direction the situation was heading. In the distance, the waxing and waning sound of sirens cut through the night.

Chen glared at Jacob. "Now your military friend is an issue."

Chapter 34: Those Prying Eyes

Smells of salt, dirt, and dead fish assaulted Mac's senses. She pressed her back against the warm steel of a cargo container. Sirens began to wail in the distance despite the authorities' agreement to not use them.

Well, there goes the element of surprise.

She tried to listen for footsteps or conversations but could only hear the pumping of her own blood through her ears. Gaining the nerve to look again, Mac inched to the corner of the container.

Just a quick peek ... see where they are. I swear if they are right around the corner I'll scream. No one is going to hear me or make it in time if they are there. Gathering her nerve, she began a countdown. One ... two ... thr—

A large arm encircled her, locking her arms to her side, as a hand clamped over her mouth in a tight seal, dragging her backward. She tried to scream but couldn't. She was pulled firmly into a solid chest. She kicked backward.

"Ow! Red," a man whispered in her ear, "it's me."

Recognizing his voice, Mac froze.

"That hurt," Cameron whispered. "And you were supposed to wait in the car." He dropped his hand from over her mouth.

"You were going the wrong way," Mac whispered sharply back. "Besides, I was just seeing where one of the containers was going. The man from the village is there, the one who put the bag on your head. From what I could hear, the leader is a guy named Chen. The big guy is Bai, and I don't know the little guy's name yet. I think they are Chen's bodyguards."

"Great work, Nancy Drew. You're going to get yourself killed one of these days." He loosened his hold enough so she could turn and face him. He seemed angry; only lucky for her, distracted by the situation at hand.

He moved in front of her and peered around the corner. "The group is starting to scatter. Dammit, I told the cops not to use their sirens."

Mac squeezed next to Cameron and looked around the corner under his chin. She just made out the African running into the cargo maze, followed by Jacob. The bodyguards had Chen's arms and were leading him away, the same way secret service officers led a president away from danger. Flashing lights appeared in the distance bouncing off the ships and containers like a light show.

"Good," she said. "The police are on their way." As the words left her mouth, she felt Cameron leave her side.

"What are you doing?" Mac grabbed for his shirt. She managed to get hold for a second, causing him to face her. "Let the police find them!"

"Stay here, Mac," Cameron ordered. He brushed her hand away. "*Do not* follow me. Wait right here for the police." He turned and ran between a row of containers in the direction Gacoki and Jacob had gone.

"No! Let the authorities handle it!" He either didn't hear her or didn't reply. The sirens didn't seem any closer either. She waited for what seemed like minutes. The sound of yelling, then the screeching of tires startled her.

"Cameron?" Mac called out, then waited. "Cameron?" Mac waited several seconds. She looked around and realized she was alone and just as vulnerable here as anywhere.

"Aw, screw it," she said to herself and ran after Cameron. "If he wants obedience, he can get a dog."

Chapter 35: Friends Suck

The bright lights of the shipyard created pockets of black shadows. Cameron ran with ease, his breath steady and his adrenaline pumping. He'd been able to catch glimpses of Jacob between the containers, knowing if he didn't catch up soon, he would lose him in the maze.

Pushing himself to go faster, Cameron was rewarded with the sight of Jacob's back disappearing behind a red container. He pushed himself to his top speed, running past the three containers he remembered seeing when he found the truck.

Taking a chance, he turned and went toward the direction of the truck in a roundabout route. He saw Jacob standing to his right, looking away from him, and seemingly stumped about which direction to run. Quietly and quickly, Cameron closed the gap between them. Once in range, he leapt.

At that same moment, Jacob turned toward him. His eyes widened as he tried to jump out of the way.

"Stop!" Cameron crashed into Jacob with a tackle good enough for the NFL. He missed Jacob's torso but was able to grab him around his thighs. Both men tumbled to the hard pavement. Loose pebbles and debris scraped his skin, adding to the wounds from his first run-in with Jacob. His elbow hit the ground hard and went numb for a few seconds, though he managed to keep his grip on Jacob.

"Dammit, Captain!"

Jacob tried to scramble away, pulling himself across the pavement with his arms, but Cameron quickly climbed onto Jacob's back. He then yanked him upward in a backbend, as he wrapped an arm around his neck, locking it with his elbow. Jacob immediately wedged his arm between Cameron's arm, stopping his attempt for a choke hold. Jacob was just as big as Cameron and equal in battle knowledge. The two struggled for dominance.

"Let me talk to you!" Cameron shoved Jacob's face to the ground, then pinned one of Jacob's arms behind his head. Using a martial arts technique, Cameron locked his legs around Jacob's torso.

"You're not taking me to jail," Jacob spit out through his clenched jaw. Wriggling, Jacob loosened Cameron's grip and attempted to break free. Cameron reestablished his tight hold by drawing Jacob closer.

"I'm not taking you to jail. I want you to work for me," Cameron yelled as he completed the pinning move. Jacob struggled for a moment then slumped. Cameron remained alert in case Jacob's intention was to catch him off guard.

"Why would you want me to work for you? I'm the bad guy, right?" Jacob's face was red from the struggle and the constricted position. Though he was concerned about Jacob passing out, he knew not to loosen his hold.

"Look. You got screwed. It happens! But you are a marine. You are better than this. And besides, what better way to get poachers than to hire one?"

Jacob said nothing, which meant he was either contemplating or buying time that neither one really had.

"Once the cops are here, I'll have no choice but to hand you over." Cameron was getting annoyed because the right option was so obvious.

"I'm in too deep. If I try to get out, I'm as good as dead," Jacob barked back.

"Whatever it is, I can help." A crunching noise distracted Cameron. A black car was headed their way at a fast speed.

That's not the good guys ... no flashing lights.

Jacob flexed, and before Cameron could brace himself, he used the distraction to flip his body left and out of Cameron's hold. They both stood as the car skidded sideways to a stop and the window started to open. Jacob grabbed Cameron and pulled him so close he could smell sweat and the bitter tang of tobacco on Jacob's breath.

"I'm sorry, but this is for your own good," Jacob growled into Cameron's ear.

Agonizing pain erupted in Cameron's gut. He looked down as Jacob pulled the knife from his belly.

"You stabbed me!"

Jacob drew Cameron close until his lips were next to Cameron's ear. "Lie here and play dead if you don't want them to shoot you. I didn't stab you that bad, but the blood will look like it."

Cameron looked disbelievingly at Jacob, then beyond him to the car's open window. A gun receded back into the dark interior. With the care of a father setting his child to sleep in a crib, Jacob guided Cameron quickly to the ground.

"I'll get you back for this," Cameron spat through gritted teeth.

"I have no doubt of that ... now shut up." Jacob stood reached into his pocket, grabbed a bandana, and made a show of wiping blood from the knife as he walked toward the car.

That S.O.B stabbed me! And now I need to play dead and hope his friends don't decide to put a bullet in me for good luck. I hope he knows what he's doing, or I am dead.

Cameron watched Jacob through the crack of an eyelid as he walked up to the car's open window. His gut burned as his own warm blood soaked his shirt, making it hard to keep still. He fought the urge to apply pressure to the wound and made his body go limp.

Jacob seemed to be purposely keeping his body between Cameron and the car. Or maybe Cameron just hoped Jacob was. He was putting all his faith in their military bond of brotherhood.

"He's dead, so put that thing away." Jacob sounded cold and calm. "I told you I could handle it. We don't need the police hearing gunshots."

A man in the car replied, "Well, let's hope he's dead, for your sake. Now hurry. Get in."

Jacob got in the car. Cameron didn't chance moving as the car sped away.

When he felt it was safe, he looked down. His shirt was soaked red, but the blood wasn't gushing out of him, meaning no major arteries were cut. *Only a true friend would stab you for your own good,* he chuckled to himself.

It hurt to laugh.

Chapter 36: I Got You, Babe

A black sedan drove past Mac at an alarming speed. She had witnessed the whole thing, helplessly watching Jacob stab Cameron then stroll to the car as if nothing of significance had happened. She wanted to run to Cameron, but her feet felt frozen to the ground. Her head spun. A feeling of disconnectedness washed over her. The lighted dock was replaced with night as her vision tunneled.

Two worlds crossed. She was back in Texas, back at the sanctuary, back to the night she found her lover dead in the lion enclosure. The big male lion, Thor, lay beside Keene. One giant paw rested protectively over him as Thor licked his head with his huge pink tongue. Keene's normally soft hair was matted and a darker brown—because it was wet from the lion licking him—from eating him.

Tears streamed down Mac's cheeks. The bodies of Cameron and Keene flicked back and forth, as if two realities converged in a repetitive loop from hell. Both men, reposing like discarded rag dolls, not moving, laughing … laughing?

The sound of laughter brought Mac's mind to the present. She made her feet move so she could get to ... *Keene … no, Cameron. I'm at a port in Kenya and not in Texas. The man on the ground is Cameron.*

She reached Cameron, then rolled him over. When he opened his eyes, she screamed.

"I'm fine," Cameron coughed out in a laugh.

"You're alive!" Mac grabbed his shoulders with force. "Why are you laughing?"

"Ow! Easy," he groaned. "Because I'm alive. I'm fine. I didn't mean to scare you."

Focusing on his midsection and his blood-soaked hands, she scolded, "Fine? You're not fine. Your bleeding ... a lot!"

"Jacob stabbed me."

"He what? He could have killed you."

"If Jacob had wanted to kill me, he would have. He had to do something, or they would have shot me."

Mac struggled to land on an emotion. She felt relief, anger, and confusion.

He lifted his shirt. The cut looked like the smile of a crazed clown. "See, the knife barely went in." He pulled the skin apart slightly and fresh blood oozed from the wound.

Mac turned away.

"Hey, I'm okay." Cameron went to touch her face. She flinched away from his red fingers. "Oh, sorry." He wiped them off in his shirt. "I really am okay. He didn't hit any organs." Cameron the twisted grin of a middle school boy who had just shown a worm to a girl.

He doesn't know what this has done to me. He thinks I'm crying for him ... it's so much more than that. She shook her head, as if to erase the memory of Keene. Mac felt the urge to hold Cameron, to kiss his face, to cry. No, she wanted to hold Keene. Cameron was not Keene. No one would be.

She debated on telling him what she had gone through, only it was still too painful to share. Instead, she managed three words.

"You're an idiot."

She took off her jacket and her top layer shirt, leaving herself in a tank top. She balled up the shirt then pushed it firmly on Cameron's wound.

He grunted, "Thanks. I owe you a shirt."

"You owe me more than that." She looked up. His eyes were focused on her. Before she could back away, he filled the gap between them and kissed her.

Mac was stunned by the warmth of his tongue in her mouth. But she wasn't thinking of Cameron, and she didn't kiss him back. Cameron released her, his eyebrows drawn together enough to make a line across the bridge of his nose.

"I need—" Mac started to explain,

Two policemen came rushing to them. "Don't worry, it's going to be okay," one of them stated.

Is it? Mac asked herself. *Will it ever be?*

Chapter 37: No Revenge

Gacoki was underwater, swimming in a sea of black and trying to get to the surface, but his hands wouldn't move. His head throbbed and his ears had an annoying ringing in them. He could hear muffled voices.

Voices? Not drowning; trying to wake up. He smelled blood. *Is that my blood?*

Gacoki tried to open his eyes. He couldn't open his left eye and could barely crack open his right one.

My knees. Why am I looking at my knees?

His neck ached, and some instinct told him to stay still. As the ringing in his ears dissipated, voices became clearer.

"I don't care how much you beat him. I want to know who he's working for."

"What does it matter?" said another person.

"Get the water."

Two. There are two people.

Heavy footsteps walked away from him, and Gacoki wondered where he was and who the men were. He remembered running at the docks and then an image of his truck came to mind. He had reached the truck and had opened the driver's side door ... then his memory went blank. Someone must have hit him from—

Freezing water drenched him. Gacoki cried out, no longer able to feign unconsciousness. His head rolled side to side violently, uncontrollably, as his muscles twitched, and pain peaked to an excruciating level.

Can't breathe!

He tried to suck in air. He told himself he must maintain control and managed a quick breath then another and another. The pain decreased from sharp to throbbing. His eye focused on cans and dishes. He was in a stock room.

"Who are you working for?" Chen stepped in front of his view, just inches from Gacoki's face. Chen's spit showered his cheek. His usual calm demeanor had been replaced by a red-faced mad man.

Gacoki stared back in silence. *I'm going to die. I'm going to die without avenging my family. I have failed.*

"I will ask again," Chen spoke deliberately, "Who … are … you … working for?"

Large hands fell hard on Gacoki's shoulders, and he was aggressively shaken. Then Bai appeared from behind him, raised his meaty hand, and slapped him. Gacoki felt stinging pain, though not as painful as before. Either the freezing water had numbed him to the pain, or he was close to death.

Bai raised his hand again.

"Stop," Gacoki croaked, and Bai lowered his hand. "No more. I'm working for no one."

"Liar!" screamed Chen.

A burst of pain shot through his jaw. He heard a *crack*.

He busted my jaw. I can't do this much longer. A multitude of regrets rushed through his mind. *I should have started a family. I should have taken my father's death as a sign from God to do better. Now I have failed, and the family name dies with me.*

"I've asked around about you, Gacoki." Chen's voice was behind him now, his breath prickled the hairs on his neck as he says, "Seems you've kept the family tradition alive. Which is not something I can say about your father."

Gacoki involuntarily flinched at the mention of his father.

"Your father used to be a big hunter, I heard. I believe he worked for one of my cartels. He also died on a hunt. Bad luck, but that's the business." Chen knelt in front of him, their dark-brown eyes locked in hate. "I can respect the whole honor thing, but your interference has now cost me money. You know that cargo we just dropped off? Guess what boat the authorities are looking at? Now tell me who hired you."

"You ... will kill ... me," he spit the words out, blood mixed with saliva.

"On *my* honor. I am a man of my word. I will not kill you," Chen responded softly, as if the offer was the most reasonable of situations.

"Go to hell," Gacoki growled.

Bai stepped forward and punched him in the liver.

The air left his lungs, and he struggled to breathe again. The pain was unbearable.

"Who hired you?" Chen asked again. His voice eerily calm now.

Please God. Just let me die. The pain is too much. I cannot go on.

"You're a fool," Chen said. Bai snorted a laugh. "I'm an honorable, rational man, and I'll ask you one last time for the name of your benefactor."

If Chen is lying, I'm dead. If he isn't lying, I may get another chance to kill him. What do I care if he knows who pays me? No one has shown me loyalty, why should I.

"How do I know you won't kill me?"

"I guess you don't." Chen lit a cigarette. He came close and blew smoke slowly in his face. The smoke burned his eyes and cuts; however, the scent of apple and diesel were pleasant.

Dagga, he thought. He took a deep breath to inhale the marijuana, hoping to dull his pain.

"Oh, you like?" Chen took another drag and blew it in his face. Gacoki took another deep breath and felt calmer.

"That's Malawi Gold," said Chen. "Finest cannabis in Africa."

Reality started to thicken as he felt the drug do its job. The pain also started to fade. *This dagga is strong.*

"Gacoki, my friend," Chen spoke softly as he took another drag, then blew it in his opened mouth again. "Just tell me, who's paying you. Why are you here?"

Maybe Chen won't kill me if I answer him. Maybe he will let me go. Though he really didn't believe that to be true.

"I was paid to tell him about the ivory. He wants to stop the elephants from dying."

"Who? Who wants to save the elephants?"

Through the smoky haze, he could see Chen looking at him intently. "I'll live? On your word?"

"On my word; I will not kill you."

"He's called Chimp."

"What the hell, Chen?" Jacob entered the room. "What are you doing to him?"

"Making him talk," Bai replied flatly.

"Did you have to pulverize him?" Jacob looked Gacoki up and down.

"It worked," Chen said. "His boss is Chimp, that old eccentric animal rights activist who has that ranch in Congo." Chen offered his joint to Jacob. "Never figured the old man would have the balls to hire an assassin."

"Pass." Jacob looked at Gacoki and chuckled. "So, the good guy hired himself a bad guy."

"Probably looking for me," Chen answered.

Gacoki wondered why Chen would think Chimp would worry about a man of Chen's status. He felt as if he was missing something important.

Jiang walked in, and Chen spun to address him. "Well?"

"They found the cargo, Mr. Lin."

"Dammit." Chen turned and slapped Gacoki. "You cost me three million!"

"I cost you nothing," Gacoki slurred back. "It's your American friend who was followed there by the other two Americans."

Chen pivoted quickly to face Jacob.

"I got the cargo to the drop off," Jacob spoke calmly. "Doesn't matter now. Your plan was figured out before we picked it up."

"Mr. Lin, Chimp has property with his own elephants," Jiang stated.

"Yeah, but it's protected by a few rangers, high powered rifles, and drones," Jacob added warily."

"Find locals and go get my ivory from his herd," Chen ordered. "Kill all of them if you have to. Consider it repayment for the loss of my shipment."

"Are you serious?" Jacob asked. "You want me to take a bunch of untrained men out to battle trained rangers? Do you think I'm stupid?"

"No, I pay you to do a job. I pay you a lot. You're the only one who needs to come back. Now go do your job. Be in and out before they can even get to you."

"What about him?" Jacob asked, pointing at Gacoki.

"He won't be an issue." Bai withdrew a gun from a holster on his belt.

At that moment Gacoki knew he was going to die. Everything was for nothing. *The Dragon wins again.*

"Hold on, mate," Jacob said flatly. "I have a few more questions."

Chen nodded, and Bai placed his gun back in its holster.

"You promised me I would live," Gacoki whimpered. He fought back tears. *I will not die a coward or crying like a child.* His face throbbed. *I will die with honor.*

"I promised *I* wouldn't kill you." Chen smiled.

"I need your boys to get me fire power," Jacob stated.

Chen pointed at Bai and Jiang. "Go. Get Jacob what he needs."

"And make sure to get me guns that work," Jacob yelled behind them as they left. "Not that made in China crap," he snorted, amused by his own joke.

"I'm sure you can handle him from here." Chen motioned to Gacoki as if he were nothing but trash that needed disposal. "Do what needs to be done once you have your information."

"No problem. I expect a bonus."

"Of course you do." Chen walked out, leaving Jacob and Gacoki alone.

Jacob's big American face came into view as he bent and peered into Gacoki's one opened eye. "You think those guys went a little overboard?"

Gacoki only stared at him, resigned to his fate.

"You were so close, little buddy. Didn't even know how close." Jacob took out a military grade pistol and drew back the safety. "You were chasing a ghost. You were never going to find *the* Golden Dragon. He's been dead for over seven years. However, the business runs in the Lin family."

"What are you saying?" Gacoki rasped. Then like a light switching on, he figured it out.

A gunshot rang through the storage room.

Chapter 38: Fancy Not Meeting You Here

The hospital in Mombasa resembled a Southern plantation house on the outside, yet was modern, crisp, and bright white on the inside. Mac and Cameron answered questions from the local police. Cameron gave the police descriptions of everyone except Jacob. In all the excitement, Mac hadn't gotten the car's license plate info, though she had provided the police a description of the car. She hoped it would be easy enough to find, considering it was nicer than most of the local cars. After the police were satisfied, they left Mac and Cameron alone.

Cameron was stripped from the waist up, with his lower torso wrapped tightly in a white bandage. Mac couldn't help admiring his tan muscle definition.

"Why do you protect him?" she asked.

"Who?"

Mac knew he was being evasive. "Jacob. You don't even like him."

"You would have to have been in the military to understand."

"To understand what, Cameron? That he poaches defenseless animals and stabs people?"

"He also helped me." Cameron's sighed and looked at her impatiently.

"Helped you?" Mac crossed her arms. "You've been held at gunpoint, abandoned unconscious in a shed, and now stabbed. If I knew your bar for friendship was so low, I would make less of an effort."

"Do you make an effort?" he smirked.

"You know what I mean." Mac dropped her arms to her sides in frustration, then started to pace the room. She wanted answers, not games. "You think your looks and charm can win any argument ... not with me."

"No, I don't think that. Please do expand on the looks and charm, though."

"It wasn't a compliment, and you're avoiding my question." Mac grew tired of his obscure flirting at the worst times.

"I know Jacob's not exactly on our team, but you're either a marine or dead. There's no in-between. I think he wants out and can't see a way."

"And you do?"

"Kill the Dragon," Cameron answered flatly.

"You mean arrest him?"

"Yeah, that would work too." His look reminded Mac of a spoiled child. She didn't like this side of Cameron, a colder side, a side blinded by some bro-code he felt obligated to follow no matter what. He was putting too much faith into Jacob, trusting he honored the same code.

"Cameron, we need—" the door opened.

"You are free to ... go" The doctor paused in the doorway, seeming to pick up on the tension in the room. Clearing his throat, he started again, "Um, you are free to go, Mr. Stephenson. You are a lucky man to require only stitches. You were less than inches away from a very serious injury."

Cameron looked at Mac, as if to say I told you so. Mac shook her head. "I'm glad I have different friends. I'm going to find something to drink while you sign all your discharge forms."

"Bring me one too," Cameron called after her.

Without a response, Mac left in search of sugar, caffeine, and carbonation. The hospital was a maze of corridors. She found herself back in the admitting area. The place was full of crying and moaning people. She walked past a man coughing and sweating bullets.

Yuck. Who knows what that guy has, but I don't want it.

Soon, she recognized the hallway they had walked earlier to the assessment area for intakes. This area was busy, too, mostly with staff. But one man stood out.

That's Jacob! He was walking in her direction, looking off to the side. Knowing that her red hair made her as easy to spot as Jacob's model good looks, she quickly ducked behind an orderly who was pushing a cart of medical equipment.

What is he doing here? she wondered. She glanced around the orderly and watched as Jacob peered in a curtained area, then stepped inside.

He didn't see me. Mac exhaled in relief. Slowly, she made her way toward the curtained area he had stepped into. Jacob's military boots were facing a bed. He spoke so softly that Mac could barely hear him.

Anticipating Jacob leaving any second, Mac positioned herself directly behind him and stared at his shoes. Since the curtain opening was at the foot of the bed, she would have about two seconds to get behind the curtain for the adjacent bed if he moved. *Hopefully, if someone was in there, they are asleep.*

"... you're safe now, Gacoki." Jacob said. "Get patched up and then go home."

Gah-coke-ee ... Gacoki ... must remember the name. I wonder if he is speaking to the man from the village and the port.

"Why ... did you ... help me?" a raspy voice mumbled. "You didn't shoot me."

Jacob was going to shoot him?

"I'm okay with killing animals ... I'm not okay with killing humans unless it's in a fair battle. Now that Chen knows Chimp hired you, I have a very delicate situation on my hands. He's going to want revenge."

Chimp hired him? Chimp hired Gacoki to do what? Does this mean they are going to kill more elephants?

"Now do yourself a favor and don't be seen again," Jacob said. "Otherwise, you'll put me in another bad spot." Jacob's shoes turned quickly.

Mac stifled a scream and froze like an antelope in a clearing after catching the scent of a lion. She had no idea what Jacob would do if he found her, and she didn't want to find out either. The curtain burst open and billowed around Mac.

To her relief, Jacob never saw her. His footfalls faded with each second. Mac released a breath she didn't know she was holding.

That had been a close call, I need to tell Cameron ... but first I want to know if the person he is talking to is the same man from the village.

Finding the seam of the curtain, she slowly pulled it back, just enough for a peek at the man Jacob had spoken to. She quickly deduced that staying hidden didn't matter because he had his eyes closed and seemed to be asleep. Quietly, Mac slid inside the curtained room to get a closer look. He was barely recognizable, one whole half of his face was swollen and bruised. She leaned in closer and was able to recognize him as the man from the village and the docks. *Gacoki ... Jacob called him.*

Dried blood was caked on his clothes and in his hair. His breathing was labored, although steady. He had obviously not been there for long since the staff hadn't cleaned the blood off his face.

Did Jacob do that? No, he couldn't have done this to him. Why would he have brought him to the hospital? Chen and his goonies must have beat that man.

An image of Amahle, the pregnant elephant, and the herd came to mind. Mac had a bad feeling in the pit of her stomach. *What if they went after her herd, for revenge?*

A cold hand grabbed hers and she had to stifle another scream as she looked down and saw dark skinny fingers lightly wrapped around her wrist. Gacoki was staring at her with one eye, the sclera red from broken vessels. Mac didn't try to pull her hand away.

Gacoki's lips moved, and a raspy sound came from them.

"I'm sorry," she managed to whisper. "I didn't hear you."

He let go of her hand, to which she was grateful, and waved for her to come closer. She hesitated but reasoned with herself that if Chimp had hired him, then he must be on the good guy's side. Plus, he was too weak to hurt anyone. She leaned towards him.

"The elephants," he wheezed, "are in danger."

"What? Are you saying the elephants at Chimp's ranch?"

Gacoki nodded his head slowly. He grabbed her hand again, as if to ensure she didn't flee. This time, his touch was weaker, his eyes were heavy, as if consciousness wasn't going to be an option for long.

"What? What is it, Gacoki?"

"The Dragon's dead. Now is the time for *mwana*."

"What? What does *mm-wha-na* mean?"

His eyes fluttered. She leaned closer to his face. Copper and a smell of rancid bile caused her to involuntarily wrinkle her nose.

"Please, tell me who is the Dragon."

"Mwana."

"Was it one of the men at the pier?"

But he didn't answer; he was unconscious. She went to shake him. The curtain quickly slid aside, the metal rings clacking against the rod. To Mac's relief, a nurse stood, just as surprised to see her.

"Who are you? I'm assuming not family." He looked at her, eyes narrowing.

"Um, a friend. Do you know what *mm-wha-na* means in English?"

"Yes," the nurse looked down, checking the IV in Gacoki's hand. "It means son. Can you tell me about what happened to this man?"

Mac left before he looked back up.

Chapter 39: All I Got Was This T-Shirt

Mac ran into Cameron's room. He was sitting up, gingerly putting on a pink T-shirt stating, "I Love Mombasa". The *M* in Mombasa was depicted as the elephant tusk arches over the downtown road.

"A nurse came by and didn't approve of the state of my shirt." Cameron's shrugged his shoulders. "This was the only thing that would fit me from the lost and found. I think I can pull off pink, and I am so ready to be out of here. Hey … where are the drinks?"

"I saw Jacob," she blurted. "And I never found a vending machine."

"What? Where?"

"He's gone. Dropped off that guy he was at the village with. I heard Jacob call him, Gacoki. He looks in real bad shape."

"Jacob?"

"No, Gacoki. His face is all banged up, and he told Jacob that Chen had found out Chimp hired him. Why would Chimp hire Gacoki?"

Cameron raised his eyebrows. "He must be an inside man, maybe for information. That's the only way Chimp would not have told me about him."

"There's more. He said something about the Dragon is dead and the son … I think he meant the Dragon is someone's son."

"Well, I'm sure he's someone's son."

"That's what Gacoki told me."

"You spoke to him? Are you mad! You could have been killed."

"He could barely move, Cameron."

Cameron paused, then raised his eyebrows in an "ah ha" moment. "Maybe the dad passed away and the son took over. We've been chasing a ghost. Did he say anything else?"

"Before he passed out, he said our elephants are in trouble. I bet it is revenge for interfering. Cameron, we have to get back!"

"I'll call Chimp," Cameron stated. "Have him put the rangers on alert and tell Bruce to get the plane ready, now."

"While you're at it, why don't you ask him why he hired Gacoki."

"I'll save that one for when we get back."

Mac grabbed Cameron's boots and accidentally threw them at him a little harder than she meant to.

"*Oof.*" Cameron caught and held onto the boots, for a moment, his eyes were squeezed shut as he took deep breaths.

"I'm sorry ... I forgot. Your *friend* stabbed you."

"Yeah, I get the sarcasm," Cameron grunted. "Let's hurry and get out of here. We need to grab our stuff at the hotel and get back to the ranch."

Chapter 40: On the Plane Again

With their car still at the port, they taxied to the hotel and changed. By the time the driver pulled up to the entrance of a charter terminal, it was 8:00 a.m.

Cameron stiffly stepped out of the car as Bruce walked up.

"Whoa, mate. What happened to you?" Bruce's eyes widened as he looked at Cameron.

"He was stabbed," Mac blurted. "But don't worry, it was by his friend."

"Been there, done that, mate."

Cameron shrugged. "It's not that bad."

"Sure, I get stabbed at least three times a year in Australia. Sounds like you had a successful weekend."

The smell of beer wafted from Bruce's breath and there was a redness to his eyes that said he was interrupted from sleeping off a good night at the pub. Mac felt like she should be worried, but right now, she didn't care. She just wanted to get back to the ranch.

While Bruce grabbed their bags, Mac helped Cameron to the plane. He leaned lightly against her, one arm around her shoulders. She looked up and he gave her a weak smile. Dark circles had formed under his eyes. *He must be exhausted,* she thought.

As they reached the tarmac, Mac couldn't believe she felt relieved to see the plane.

"Yesterday you couldn't pay me to get on that flying death trap you call a plane. Today, just knowing it has wings, is good enough for me."

Bruce didn't look surprised. "Yeah, I kinda heard about your adventure." Both Mac and Cameron looked at him, as he motioned behind him with his thumb. "We have a third passenger. I think you know him."

Kendalie appeared from behind the plane and walked up to them. "I heard you may need some help." He gently took one of the bags from Mac.

Mac was both relieved and suspicious. With so many lies going on, she didn't know if she could trust him.

"What did you find out?" Kendalie asked.

"You first. What happened to the ship?" Mac replied.

"Chimp called me and told me about your incident at the port and to meet you here." Kendalie looked at Cameron. "We are working closely with the Chinese government, and they are searching the containers for the ivory. I've not received official word, yet."

"There were three, by the dialect, Chinese men and ... and one other," Cameron reported. "A man named Gacoki. I believe he's African ... I don't know what region."

Kendalie's face was stone still, but his eyes flicked left for an instant.

Was that a look of recognition? Does he know Gacoki? Mac assumed he did. She turned to Cameron to see if he had noticed. She was startled to see him bent over and holding his side. "Are you okay?"

"Getting out of the car pulled the stitches. Hurts." He stood up straight, sucking in his breath.

"You need to get horizontal for a couple of days, mate. Let that heal. Let's get you on that plane."

Mac climbed in the back, while Kendalie and Bruce helped Cameron sit in the front. Once they were all onboard, Bruce started the engine, then reached behind him into a small bag behind the seat, pulled out a beer and handed it to Cameron.

"He's on medication," Mac raised her voice to be heard over the engine.

"This'll make it work better." Bruce flashed a yellow-toothed smile that told of many nights of pubs, beer, and cigarettes.

"Or he'll lose a kidney," she answered.

"That's why you have two." Bruce shook his head. "You worry too much. It's my last beer anyway. One won't kill him."

Mac rolled her eyes and buckled her seatbelt.

Sweat had begun to drip from Cameron's head. He took the beer, cracked the tab, then guzzled it down, concluding it with a large belch.

"Perfect. Maybe it'll help me sleep." Cameron looked at Mac. "You, okay?"

"Just peachy."

"I've never understood that American saying," Bruce yelled over the noise of the engine as he put his headset on. "I mean a peach is pink and fuzzy, or bald, depending on the peach. Just doesn't make sense."

"In this case," Mac answered, "it means I'm sweaty, dirty, mad, and sitting behind a half-buzzed idiot about to fly the plane I'm in."

"Ah, well, that's definitely not what I imagined it meant." Bruce blushed, then pushed the throttle in. The plane started rolling down the runway.

Cameron's head was loose, and he seemed to be falling asleep. Mac worried he would hit his head on the window. She was about to look for a blanket or a cushion when she noticed Kendalie take off his jacket and set it between the window and Cameron's head. This small gesture took away whatever mistrust she had with Kendalie.

Soon, the bumpy ground was replaced by smooth air and the feeling of weightlessness. Within minutes Mac slipped into sleep as exhaustion took over. She just hoped Bruce was sober enough to stay awake.

Chapter 41: Oh, Sheila

The wooden roller coaster jostled Mac from side to side as it headed to the top of the track. The wheels made a slow and torturous click-clack, click-clack. She was excited yet had a nervous feeling in the pit in of her stomach. Cameron was there in the front seat with her. He was laughing. They reached the top, and to her horror, the tracks were gone halfway down the drop. Cameron kept laughing and lifted his hands up in the air.

The cart paused as it peaked at the top. Mac hoped it would stop. Instead, it started to roll over the top of the arch, then quickly picked up speed as they plummeted to the missing track. Cameron was still smiling, though his face had gone pale, his eyes glassy. There was flesh missing from his cheeks, and she could see his teeth.

Mac woke with a start. A wave of nausea hit her as she felt a small drop. Disoriented, she peered out the plane's window. The sky shone a bright orange line on the horizon, blanketed by a deep purple from the oncoming of a darkening sky. They were close to the treetops. Another sensation of dropping made her stomach lurch again. She had slept the entire flight. They were getting ready to land on the grass airstrip back at the ranch.

"Good evening, Sleeping Beauty," Cameron teased from the front. "Nice drool mark."

Bruce snorted a laugh as Kendalie tried to politely hide his smile.

Mac's cheeks flushed as she quickly wiped a large wet patch from her cheek and controlled her urge to vomit. Doing that would be more embarrassing than drooling.

"Home sweet home," Bruce called from the front.

The ranch came quickly into view as the plane coasted down, then bounced onto the grass field.

Cameron let out small grunts.

"Sorry, mate," Bruce apologized. "Not exactly Chicago O'Hare airport out here."

"Not your fault. Looks like it's time for more meds."

The plane soon parked, and everyone debarked. Cameron gingerly stepped out of the plane. His movements were stiff; however, his eyes had a glint that indicated the rest did him good and he was ready for anything.

"Kendalie, my friend," Chimp exclaimed walking up to greet them.

"Good to see you in person, my friend." Kendalie stepped up to Chimp. They shook hands and embraced each other with genuine enthusiasm and love that longtime friends share.

"I've missed you," Chimp said to Kendalie. "Has it been almost a year since we've seen each other?"

"Whatever it has been, it has been too long." Kendalie's eyes looked wet and on the verge of tears.

"Ah, before I forget … your people called while you were en route. They said it was urgent that you call them. You can use the phone in my office."

Kendalie replied, "Maybe this call will be good news. We are working closely with the Chinese government, which has been better about supporting our efforts. Cameron and Mac have been very useful. We now have names and faces to track down instead of ghosts."

"That's great news! I apologize I couldn't join you on location," Chimp stated breathlessly. Mac noticed his pallor was off and he looked unwell.

"Come, this way." Chimp gestured and started walking. "I have food, and we can plan our next move. Bruce, did you want to join us?"

"No sir. I need to crash. I'd appreciate some of that food though."

"I'll have a big plate sent to your room. You can stay in one of the guest rooms."

"Appreciate it, mate. I know the place. Have a g' night, all."

"Thanks, Bruce." Mac tilted her head, her voice softening. "Really. Thanks for keeping us safe."

"Careful, I might think ya trust my flying skills," Bruce warned her as he walked towards his room.

"Let's not go that far," Mac yelled after him.

Chimp focused on Cameron who was gingerly holding his side. "How are you? You've looked worse, but not by much."

"He was stabbed by a friend," Mac injected as she, Cameron, and Kendalie followed him. Chimp looked at Cameron with a raised eyebrow.

"One of the poachers is a Marine," Cameron explained. "His name is Jacob, and I served with him. He's the one who stabbed me, and I should add that if he hadn't, I would have been shot."

"If he hadn't what?" Chimp asked.

"Stabbed me." He now received a perplexed look from Kendalie. "Jacob stabbed me to save me from one of Chen's meatheads putting a bullet in me."

After a brief pause, Mac looked at Chimp. "Chen's pissed and planning to get more ivory quickly. Our herd's in danger. The entire herd."

"How do you know this?" Chimp asked.

"I overheard Jacob. He happened to be in the same hospital Cameron was in. He brought in another man, Gacoki."

Mac noticed Kendalie and Chimp exchanged a brief look. She was ready for all this secrecy to be done.

Hopefully, dinner would be quick. She was anxious to see Fenny.

Chapter 42: Dinner and a Show

As Bruce split and went to the guest room, Mac and Cameron entered Chimp's sitting room. Kendalie was already on the phone. It was only minutes before he finished the call then joined them.

"I have official word," he smiled, "the authorities seized almost four tons of ivory in the containers. The dock supervisor and one worker were detained. They also found rhino horns in another container. Probably unrelated ... a win none the less."

Cheers, high-fives, and praises filled the room.

"This is great news," Mac exclaimed. "Were they able to find Chen and the others?"

"No. Not yet. But they will."

Mac looked at Cameron. *Is that relief on his face that they didn't find Jacob?*

Kendalie continued, "They discovered that the ivory was being hidden in false walls within the cargo containers. Luckily, an observant officer noticed the twelve-meter-long container full of timber looked shorter on the inside. After they emptied it, they discovered a one-meter-long hidden storage area at the end wall. They're now alerting the Mombasa government and the LAGA and will request a trace. And they're searching more container ships with similar cargo."

"What is LAGA?" Mac whispered to Cameron.

"It stands for Last Great Ape organization," Cameron responded. "It's like wildlife law enforcement. It's good news for a big organization like that to get involved."

"My friends, this success is all due to your hard work," Chimp said. "Now we can really celebrate with a wonderful meal." Chimp gestured to their right.

In an adjoining room, a long, low table was adorned with dishes of colorful foods. The aroma of garlic and onion made Mac's mouth water and her stomach growl.

"The war isn't over, but a major battle has been won!" Kendalie raised a victorious fist. They all cheered again.

"Corinne has prepared *nyembwe* chicken, one of my favorites," Chimp said. Mac must have involuntarily crinkled her nose at the mention of meat because he added with a smile, "Not to worry, Mac. Corinne has prepared a mushroom version as well."

Mac sat upon a pillow, grateful for the rest. Cameron struggled to ease himself down.

"How's your pain?" asked Chimp.

"It's tolerable." Cameron smiled, then grimaced.

"This is a beautiful kuba cloth," Mac admired as she ran her hands over orange and purple triangle shapes, then traced the maze of yellow stitching with her fingertips.

"Ah, thank you. It was a gift from a member of the royal family—I won't tell you which one—we had a very lovely summer together." Chimp's eyes seemed to sparkle at a memory he wasn't sharing.

With a *pop,* Kendalie pulled the cork from a dark bottle then began to pour wine in their glasses. "This is a favorite of mine. Dodoma. It's a dry red that comes from the Dodoma region and the only red grape variety of the region of Makutupora."

"Oh, I love cabernet," Mac said excitedly.

"Then I'm sure you will love this," Kendalie exclaimed.

The aroma of apricots and chocolate filled her nose as she swirled the deep red liquid in her glass. The first taste was a little sweeter than her liking, quickly rounding into a soft grape flavor with a bitterness that didn't linger on her tongue. Overall, it was pleasant and hard not to drink quickly. She tried to pace herself because she felt that she needed to keep her guard up. But with the stress of the day, the pleasant feel of a buzz quickly affected her rational mind, and she took a second glass of wine.

The meal was a feast of fruits, nuts, rice, and stews. Mac ate and drank to her fill and then ate some more, as did everyone. The mood was light and filled with laughter.

Kendalie and Cameron reviewed the details of the past few days with Chimp, who nodded thoughtfully throughout their stories. At times, his brow furrowed in what seemed like deep contemplation or worry. Mac looked for involuntary twitches or facial expressions that could give her clues about who was telling the truth and who was lying.

I've been watching too many movies. Like I could catch anything more subtle than a seizure.

Chimp finally said, "I'm truly sorry for all the inconvenience and physical pain you have all been through. I fear some of it is my fault."

"I don't think you can take the blame in this, my friend," Kendalie stated. "No one can tell the future."

"Yes, but I've put people in danger." Chimp's eyes locked onto Mac's. "People who shouldn't be placed in danger."

"I've held my own," Mac responded. "And I haven't passed out or gotten stabbed."

"Touché," Cameron responded, as everyone chuckled.

"Yes, you've done well." Chimp stood up and the guests followed suite. "It's time for some well-deserved rest. Tougher times are ahead. Kendalie … you can stay in my other guest quarters here in my hut. Cameron … I'm sure you're good driving Mac to hers. There's a Jeep parked out front. The keys are inside."

"Not a problem." Cameron held out his arm in a gentlemanlike gesture. "My lady, your carriage awaits."

Mac wrapped her arm around his. She knew he was just being silly and dramatic, but her cheeks grew hot anyway. The alcohol had made her forgiving and more susceptible to his charm. Even with her doubts, Cameron had some kind of hold on her. She just hoped that it wouldn't cloud her judgement as much as the wine had.

Stepping outside, the fresh air was cool and smelled of grass. The Jeep wasn't far, only she had an idea. "Can you give me a second? I want to go to the bathroom. I'm sure it's nicer here."

"Yes, it actually is. Go past where we ate to the middle door. It's between the guest room and bedroom." Cameron walked away with a little swerve in his step. He pulled himself into the Jeep and started it. "I'll wait here."

Mac walked back to Chimp's hut. She quietly opened the door, careful to not make noise, then tiptoed inside. The light in the office was still on, and she could hear Kendalie and Chimp's voices. She peered in. The men, faced away from her, sat smoking cigars and drinking short glasses of a golden liquor. Mac felt wrong for spying but listened anyway. They spoke in soft tones.

"The Dragon will seek retribution. I've confirmed the information that they're coming for your herd," Kendalie stated.

"My herd? Let them come. I'll ensure they're either caught or dead. What about the man … Gacoki?"

"The assassin?" Kendalie asked flatly.

Oh my god. He hired an assassin! Mac couldn't believe what she was hearing. I was talking with an assassin.

Chimp waved off Kendalie's words with his hand. "Whatever he was, he had a job to do. He failed, and now the war has been brought to my doorstep." Chimp pinched his nose and lowered his head. "I'm sorry. That sounded cold. I'm just … tired. Are we any closer to finding the identity of the Dragon? Do we know what he may look like?"

"I know you're tired, my friend." Kendalie put his hand on Chimp's shoulder, and Mac noticed how frail Chimp looked. "We don't think he's African. Probably Chinese and in his seventies. We believe he makes his contacts and deals at a place in downtown Mombasa simply called Chinese Restaurant."

Chimp gave an amused grunt. "Clever name."

"We've investigated the clientele," Kendalie continued. "It's owned by Lin Xiu. His son Lin Chen—in China, the surname is first by the way—goes there frequently. We think Xiu's, or Mr. Lin as he goes by, is the one bringing in the business, except we have nothing to prove it."

Chen? Mac remembered that Gacoki had said mwana. Son. *If the Chen on the docks was the son of Lin Xiu's ... and the father was dead, then that would make Chen the Golden Dragon!*

"My friend," Kendalie said after a pause, "something's wrong. Not just the elephants. What is it?"

Chimp slumped in his chair. "I don't have much longer."

Kendalie nodded knowingly.

Not much longer till what? Maybe Chimp had to leave the country or maybe ...

The men stood. Mac spun, plastering her back to the wall. She frantically looked around for an escape.

"It's time for bed," Chimp said. "I'm tired."

Mac knew if she headed toward the door, they would see her before she reached the steps, instead. she tiptoe sprinted to what she hoped was the bathroom. She had to go anyway.

After she did her business and washed her hands, she headed out the bathroom door. Chimp and Kendalie were in the hall looking at her.

"Um," she said, "you might want to wait before going in there. Something didn't agree with me." Mac's ears felt hot, and her heart rate increased with the lie. The two men looked at each other, hopefully just as uncomfortable hearing her statement as she felt delivering it.

"I hope you're alright," Chimp stated.

"Yes, just glad I was near a bathroom. I've been in there awhile. Sorry about that." Mac hurried off. She half expected one of them to tackle her and ask her what she knew, but no one did. When she got to the Jeep, she jumped in, surprising a half dozing Cameron.

"Whoa," Cameron said. "I was almost asleep. What took you so long?"

"Um … you know. Food issues."

"I hope you lit a match."

"Don't be gross." Mac gave Cameron a tired look. "Just get me to my bed."

"If you insist." Cameron's face lit up in a devious grin.

"Not like that," Mac responded.

"Are you sure?" Cameron looked at her and wiggled his eyebrows up and down. Just before she could answer, he cut in, "Just kidding."

Mac didn't know whether to be angry or relieved. She was tired of this game.

Chapter 43: Don't Be a Snitch

Stars speckled the night like spilled glitter on black construction paper. The whole way to her hut, Mac sat in silence and debated how to tell Cameron that Chimp hired an assassin and her suspicions about Chen being the Golden Dragon.

The Jeep stopped in front of Mac's small hut. A dim solar-powered light glowed above the door. She was anxious to get inside and see Fenny but paused as she struggled with the impulse to tell Cameron everything. She was concerned that Cameron's relationship with Jacob and Chimp would cloud his judgement. *If I can't trust Cameron, who can I trust?*

"Are you okay?" Cameron turned off the engine.

"What? Sorry. I was thinking about everything. It's a lot to take in."

They sat in silence for a moment. "Do you trust Chimp?" she blurted.

"What? With my life, of course." Cameron studied her. "Why?"

"No reason. I just don't know him that well, and he seems to keep a lot from us."

"As any leader or boss would, we don't have to know all the details. Besides, you should feel good that he allowed you to come with me. That shows he trusts you."

"Yeah, I guess." The Jeep door opened with a *screech*. Fenny yipped from within the hut. "It's just that I heard him and Kendalie speaking when I went to go use the bathroom."

"You spied on them?"

"More like ... just happened to walk by," she lied. "Gacoki is an assassin."

Cameron's face remained neutral; his eyes opened wider for a brief second. "That *is* interesting."

"Interesting? He's a hired murderer. That's wrong."

"You know this for a fact? You could have taken it out of context."

"I know both Kendalie and Chimp know who he is. I know he's the same guy who put a bag over your head. Doesn't this concern you? That Chimp may be working outside the law."

"Red, bad guys don't follow the rules. The only way to win is to beat them at their own game."

"That may have been an answer to have while serving in the military during a war, but not here, not now. You need to follow the rules like everyone else."

Cameron shook his head. "You can't make the world better by learning about the environment, buying organic, and donating money. Someone still must do the dirty work ... pick up a gun ... face the bad guys head-on."

"Screw you! I do way more than that. It's not like I'm sitting on the sidelines here."

"I did not mean it that way. I don't want to fight."

"I don't want to fight either. I just brought it up so you would know who you're dealing with. And what do you know of Kendalie or Bruce for that matter?"

Cameron sighed. "Can we philosophize about people in the morning? I'm exhausted."

"Oh, sorry I exhaust you." Mac jumped from the Jeep and quickly headed toward her door. "Fenny is going berserk inside. I need to get to him before he gets his water everywhere."

As she reached for the doorknob, Cameron's hand gently grabbed her arm and turned her toward him, startling her. She hadn't realized he had followed.

"Dang it, Red." Cameron pulled her close, so she had to look up at his face. "You don't exhaust me. I'm just tired and I don't want to fight. I just want to—"

"You want to what?"

Sliding his hand down to her lower back, he drew her in as if to kiss her. For a moment, she was stunned, her head spun in a sea of emotions. Then, anger came flooding in a red rush as she pushed him away.

"What?" he asked. "I thought—"

"Thought what? You could just kiss me anytime you want! You're drunk, Cameron."

"I'm sorry, I just … you're right." Cameron turned away.

"No, you can't just walk away either. What's going on? What do you want from me?" Mac yelled.

"I care about you," Cameron stated.

"And?"

"And that's it."

"Enough said." Mac turned away before Cameron could see the tears forming in her eyes. She was an emotional cornucopia, mad, sad, and embarrassed, and she didn't even know why she cared. She stormed into her hut, shut the door, then flopped against it as tears rolled down her cheek.

"Wait, Red," Cameron yelled after her.

She didn't answer.

"Red?" His voice was soft. He tapped softly on the door. "I'm sorry."

"Go away," Mac cried out through tears. A heavy silence filled the next few minutes, then the Jeep's engine revved as Cameron drove off.

Fenny stood on his hind legs and whined for her to open the cage.

"I'm coming, Fenny." Mac let the small fox out. He ran around her feet then into her arms. His excitement filled her heart with the comfort only a furry companion could give. "You're the only male I trust here, Fenny."

Her mind wandered to images of Keene again. He had loved her with all his heart. They had had a special love, a special bond. One that she feared she may never find again. "Guess my one true love ticket has been used, Fenny." His golden eyes watched her. Ever so gently, he stood up on her lap, placed his little paws on her chest, and licked her nose.

Mac held him close as the emotions from the last three days left her body in shudders and tears. At some point she remembered that she didn't even tell Cameron that she believed Chen was the dragon.

Tomorrow, she promised, *tomorrow I'll go ask Chimp himself.*

Chapter 44: I Have a Secret

You just couldn't let her know you loved her, could you? Cameron admonished himself as he headed back to his quarters. He was upset with himself for hurting Mac, and angry for lying to her.

He had fallen in love with Mac not long after she had arrived. Her red hair and spunky, stubborn attitude had transfixed him. Cameron also knew they would never work—his relationships never had. The mission was always first. Love was for accountants and teachers, not soldiers. *Emotions cloud the mind.*

The Jeep's lights slowly crawled along the dirt road until his hut came into view. Abebe was sitting on the steps. Cameron wondered what he wanted so late. After Cameron parked, he forgot his injuries an jumped out. He was rewarded with a stab of pain.

Alcohol and painkillers are wearing off. I hope this is a short visit.

"Brother! I heard you were back." Abebe stood then embraced Cameron.

"Ouch. Nice to see you too."

Abebe held Cameron at arm's length. "I was going to ask you if you had a good time ... I take it you didn't. Are you hurt?"

"Stabbed. Long story."

Abebe grinned. "Oh, so you did have a good time. Maybe tomorrow after you rest, you can tell me."

"There won't be any rest tomorrow." Cameron looked around. "Come on in … I'll catch you up."

Cameron opened the door and a wave of dirty clothes odor drifted out of the dark room.

"Guess I need to do laundry." Cameron turned on a dim bedside light then pushed a pile clothes off the bed. He sat, leaning up against the wall for support as he stretched his tired, aching legs.

Abebe grabbed a wooden desk chair and sat.

"Were you able to get any closer to our spy?" Cameron asked.

Abebe played with his hat, running his fingers round and round the rim. "No. I suspect it might be one of the people, besides Lebron, who has access to the supply logs." Abebe went on, "That would be Thato, Bandile, or Siyabonga."

"How do you figure?" Cameron sat forward in anticipation.

"Lebron came to me." Abebe paused, obviously upset. "The boy said the logs were being altered, and it has been happening for several months. At first, just occasionally and only for food ... lately, it has been more frequent and now included guns. The boy was afraid he would lose his job if he was suspected, so he told me this."

"The food isn't a big deal ... the guns, however, puts all of us in danger. Hell, it could be two different people."

"We have an enemy out there, and now they may shoot us with our own guns," Abebe added.

"Cameron, as you know, Siyabonga is my nephew, so I am inclined to not suspect him."

"I understand, nevertheless we can't rule him out … yet." Cameron shook his head.

Abebe raised his head and looked deep into Cameron's eyes for a long moment before he spoke. "Yes, well he is on a day off … so I will keep an eye on the inventory to see if any goes missing. If it does, that will rule him out."

"Good, because we are expecting some unwanted company … soon."

"Oh?"

"Rumor is the Golden Dragon is going to go after our herd, since we messed up his delivery. We are going out tomorrow afternoon. We will need to be in place by the evening."

"I will ensure we are all ready," Abebe stated and stood. "Now get some rest."

"Thanks friend." Cameron scooted down onto the bed. "You, too. We won't be getting much sleep in the next few days."

Chapter 45: I Didn't Sleep at All Last Night

The sun peeked through the shades. Mac was grateful to start the day. She had slept restlessly, worried about the elephants, especially Amahle. She would deliver any day now. Once born, the calf would be slower and more vulnerable than the rest. The knowledge that poachers were on their way terrified her. She also felt conflicted with her knowledge that Chimp had hired an assassin ... and she worked for him ... and with Cameron. Who is right?

Cameron had talked of killing the Dragon, but I still don't believe the answer to death is more death. But if Chen is the Dragon, he is responsible for thousands of elephant murders. Plus, he almost killed Cameron. So why does the idea of Chimp hiring an assassin to take out the Dragon bother me?

"Because Chimp's good," she said out loud. Fenny's ears perked, and he looked at her with one eye before slowly closing it again. He nestled deeper into a warm ball at her feet.

"Chen needs to go to trial and serve time, so others will think twice about poaching," she preached to a sleeping Fenny. "There are lines in the sands of morality, otherwise there would just be chaos. And if those lines are blurred, how would I know I'm on the right side?" Mac wiggled her feet. Fenny stirred and looked up at her with hooded eyes.

"Wake up, cutie. I need to go talk to Chimp. I must know what kind of person I'm working for."

***

Mac walked quickly up the steps to Chimp's hut. She knocked and poked her head in the door to listen.

"Come in," Chimp called out. "I'm at the table."

Mac entered, expecting Kendalie to be there; only Chimp was alone. She walked in and sat on the floor next to him.

"Good morning, Mac. Anything I can help you with?" His pallor was concerning. Dark purple shown under his eyes. His light blue and gold dashiki shirt, hung on his thin body like a sack and his white linen pants also seemed too big; a stark contrast to the man she met the other day, full of energy and vitality.

"Chimp, I wanted to talk with you, about—is Kendalie here?"

"No, he went to talk with the rangers. We received disturbing information early this morning. The attack on the herd will be tonight, so Kendalie is making sure the rangers are gathered and making preparations." His brow furrowed. "What is it you need to talk to me about?"

Mac summoned up her nerve. "I know about Gacoki."

"Gacoki?" Chimp's eyebrows raised but remained silent.

"I know you hired him to find and kill the Dragon. I heard you and Kendalie talking."

"I'm disappointed you spied on us."

"I'm disappointed you hired an assassin."

"I didn't exactly seek Gacoki out," Chimp spoke softly, looking directly in her eyes. "He found me and asked for financial support. His dad, who was a poacher, was killed a long time ago. Gacoki blames the Dragon for his father's death. For taking advantage of a man trying to feed his family." His shoulders sagged. "I gave him money to support him while he looked for the Dragon, not to pay him to kill him … at least that is how I justified it in my head. It was my Hail Mary pass."

"It's wrong. You've done too much good to do something like that. What do you mean Hail Mary pass?"

Chimp seemed to deflate even more. "I know what this looks like, Mac."

"It looks like you just got tired and tried to beat them at their own game. I don't want to work for or be a part of a team that hires an assassin."

"I just wanted insurance that the ranch would be safe. If only for a little while." His eyes seemed to focus deep into hers.

"We'd all like to take the easy way out, life just isn't—

"Mac, I'm dying."

No words came to her. She hoped she had heard him wrong. She had suspected his health was bad, just not this bad.

"I have acute lymphoblastic leukemia."

"Can you—"

He held up his hand to stop her. "I have tried different treatments for years. I'm weak and exhausted. It's getting harder for me to get out of bed. It'll be soon now."

"I'm so sorry." Mac placed her hand on Chimp's. He patted it, then left his hand on top of hers. The intimacy of his warm hand on hers brought tears to her eyes.

"Oh, now … don't cry. I've had a good life and I've made my peace with it, Mac. I just want to set this ranch up for success before turning it over to Cameron. I need to feel that I haven't left him with an impossible task. The elephants will always be in danger. Except, once the Dragon is out of the picture, it will be a big step toward bringing down a major poaching ring and keeping the elephants safe."

Mac took her time before replying because she didn't want to regret her words later. "I'm going to tell you something, but you must promise that you'll do the right thing and that you'll notify the authorities and not take things into your own hands."

"What is it, Mac?"

"I think I know who the Dragon is. Or at least was."

Chimp straightened. His eyes flashed with a liveliness that wasn't there just moments before.

Mac took a deep breath and exhaled the words, "You were on the right track with Chen."

"But he's too young. The Dragon is probably in his sixties or seventies."

"Or he's dead," Mac stated matter-of-factly.

"I've been so stupid." Chimp's face paled. He pinched the bridge of his nose with his fingers.

"How do you know this?" Kendalie said from behind, making both Mac and Chimp jump. "Do you have proof?"

"No, no proof. It was just something Gacoki said. He told me the Dragon was dead, and then he said *mwana*."

"*Mwana* means, son." Kendalie sat beside Mac. "You spoke to Gacoki?"

"Yes, he was in the same hospital as Cameron. He was beaten up badly."

"You saw him there?" Kendalie asked anxiously.

"Yes. Why?"

"We cannot locate him," Kendalie sounded worried.

"You're kidding me? What would cause him to leave?" Mac ping-ponged her gaze between Chimp and Kendalie.

"Revenge." Kendalie stated flatly.

"Call him off," Mac exclaimed.

"I'm afraid it isn't up to me anymore what happens." He looked down at his feet. "Gacoki is off the grid."

The three sat in silence. Mac could hear a clock ticking from somewhere in the room.

Suddenly, Chimp jumped from his chair, "It is up to me what happens to *our* elephants!" His energy seemed to rise. "We're going to make this right! I'm meeting with everyone this morning to plan. Are you in, Mac?"

He held out his hand to help her up. She took it gingerly, helping herself up as much as she could.

"For the elephants, I'm in."

Chapter 46: Ready, Set, Fight

The main room was full. Abebe, Roshan, Thato, and Bandile were already present. They stood quietly, their postures tense, eyes wide and focused. They looked ready for a battle.

Roshan and Thato looked like brothers, both short compared to Abebe's tall frame and both with high cheek bones and gaunt frames. The only way to tell the two apart was Thato's hint of a curly beard that lined his jaw and chin contrasted with Roshan's thin mustache. Bandile matched Abebe's height, although his frame was thicker, and his cheeks were full, giving him a boyish look.

Cameron walked in the room, then stood beside Mac.

"Morning," she said.

"Morning. About last night—"

"We're good." Mac focused on everyone except him.

"I want to apologize." Cameron turned toward her, and she met his gaze.

"We're fine, Cameron. Really. Let's just focus on our herd." She had cried her feelings out last night and understood she was still mourning Keene and wasn't ready to move on.

Chimp leaned against his desk, Kendalie by his side, "Where is Siyabonga?"

"He is on his day off. There was no time to reach him," said Abebe.

"That leaves us short. Kendalie, can you help?" Chimp looked to his friend.

"Yes. I will go out with the rangers." Kendalie stood tall beside Chimp, his chest puffed like a rooster before a fight.

"The time has come," Chimp continued, "when the war has made it to our home grounds. We have information that the Golden Dragon is making a move tonight, and we need to be ready." Chimp cleared his throat and spoke louder. "They'll have rifles—this will be dangerous—but we have the technology, the passion, and the mission to protect our herd." He gestured to Cameron.

Cameron faced the group. "I've located the herd in the left quadrant of the property. The best way in for the poachers to approach is from the south. I doubt they would take the river. We'll have two teams. Team Gold, which will be Abebe, Thato, and Bandile. And Team Blue, which will be Roshan and Kendalie."

Mac stepped forward. "What about Amahle?"

"Roshan and Thato reported that she has shown signs of discomfort," Abebe answered.

"When?" Mac asked.

"Soon after you left for Mombasa," Roshan jumped in.

"Then I need to go. Someone needs to be there just in case Amahle or her baby needs help."

Thato nodded his head in agreement.

"Yes," Chimp said. "A birth will make it even more difficult to keep them safe. The other elephants will try to protect Amahle in a tight group and that will make for easy targets."

"They're sitting ducks," Mac whispered.

"The rangers will be there to protect them." Cameron put a hand on Mac's shoulder saying, "You're staying with me."

Mac glared at him. "The rangers will be busy fighting. I will stay out of the way. Plus, if it comes down to it, I can shoot."

"You've trained?" Chimp asked.

"Yes, and I'm a good shot."

"She is," Cameron sighed.

"Great." Chimp clapped his hands together. "We can use all the help we can get."

Cameron shook his head, "We aren't done talking about this." Mac only shrugged in return. "Fine, you're on team Blue."

Cameron motioned to a table with a large piece of paper on it. The group gathered around as he drew a rudimentary drawing of elephants in the middle of the white paper.

"There are rocks to the south." Cameron drew circles under the elephants. "Team Gold will hide there." He drew more circles to the left of the elephants. "There are also rocks to the east. Team Blue, you will be here." Cameron tapped his finger on the ovals. "I don't think the poachers will come from the north as they would have to cross water. The plan is to get there first and stop them before they get close enough to kill. I'll have Beetle Juice flying and keep an eye out from above."

Abebe added, "These people might be someone you know from your village. It is your job to stop them! You will not have the luxury to ask if they will surrender." Roshan, Thato, and Bandile looked warily at each other.

"Let us pray we do not," Roshan said.

Mac understood Abebe was telling them to shoot first. She didn't know if she could do it and prayed it didn't come to that.

"We need to get in position before sundown," Cameron said. "Go and get a good breakfast in you."

"May God be with all of you," Chimp addressed the group. "And thank you for your bravery."

Chapter 47: Don't Look Scared

After an uneventful breakfast, Mac went back to her hut. She needed time with Fenny and to mentally prepare for the night. She sat on her bed then pulled on her black leather boots, and slowly relaced the shoestring. Fenny sat beside her, completely fascinated with her string weaving. While she laced them up, she went through the plan in her head.

We locate the herd, get close, but not close enough to spook them. Then we sit and wait for the poachers. They will find we have surrounded them, and they will surrender. It sounds easy enough—except ... what if they don't surrender and we have to shoot? What if I have to shoot someone? No, it won't come to that ... what if it does?

"Can I do it, Fenny?"

He answered with a fanatic yip, then jumped to the floor to scuttle around the room in his daily routine of bug patrol.

"I'll take that as a yes."

But Mac wasn't so sure she could shoot someone. She didn't believe in hurting anything or anybody. *How did I get here?*

Pulling a trunk from under her bed, she opened it, taking in the scent of steel and oil as she picked up her AK-101. The old rifle was common in Africa. Originally designed for mass Armies, such as the Russian and Chinese, they flooded Africa during times of internal conflict. Cameron had given her this one. It was cool and solid in her hands.

It had been a few weeks since she last practiced, but she was good. Her mother, a single Texan mom, felt guns were as basic of a need as bread and water. She had taken Mac to the shooting range since high school; she was a natural.

Cameron had taken her natural talent and perfected it. He taught her about adjusting for wind and how to shoot targets much farther away than those at the range. With her mom, shooting had been a hobby. With Cameron, shooting had been a necessary skill. Unlike her mother, he had killed people in battle, and Mac could tell doing that changed a person. She wondered if she would feel that change tonight and if she'd be able to handle it.

She checked the chamber and ensured it was empty. Then she aimed at nothing, just felt the weight in her hands. After training with Cameron for three months, it almost scared her how comfortable the rifle felt. She could hit thirty-eight out of forty rounds in the vital zones of the targets. Cameron told her that made her an expert shot.

Of course, shooting paper was much different than a living being. She tried to visualize shooting a human. Under what circumstance would that come naturally? She was sure if her life, one of the other ranger's lives, or one of the elephant's lives depended on it, she could pull the trigger. Or rather, she liked to think she could.

Which takes more guts? Shooting or not shooting? She determined it wasn't about bravery or courage to take the shot; it was about knowing what would happen if you didn't, believing that you are right, and having the conviction you're right.

Mac turned and faced her mirror, aiming the rifle at the reflective self.

"Do you feel lucky?" She stared into her own blue eyes.

A noise came from outside the door. She turned with the gun still raised. Cameron walked in, knocking on the door as he opened it.

"Whoa there, Red!" He ducked instinctively.

"Don't worry. It's not loaded," she laughed as she immediately lowered the rifle. "Just practicing my Clint Eastwood."

Fenny burst from under the bed and circled Cameron's feet, before running again to safety.

"Well, okay there, Miss Texas. I think you got the look and the backup from your furry deputy." Cameron dug in his pocket and pulled out a green cap, "Here … I brought you this to cover that red head of yours." He straightened and paused for a second. The look on his face changed as she grabbed the hat.

"What's wrong, Cameron?" she asked as she placed the hat on her head. She admired her look in the mirror before grabbing her mag pouch and clipping it to her belt. She put three magazines in her pouch.

"Red, maybe you shouldn't go. I'm not comfortable with you out there without me." Mac retrieved a cricket from the jar and placed it in Fenny's open cage.

"You think I can't handle it?"

"No, no. That's not it at all." Cameron's words seemed to catch in his throat.

With a war cry, Fenny darted from under the bed and into the cage, bounding on the helpless green victim.

"What is it then? I won't be alone. Kendalie, Abebe, and the other rangers will be there." Mac closed the cage, then sat on her bed, and Cameron joined her. He sat close to her, and she fought the urge to move away.

"It's just," Cameron started. "I mean ... it's dangerous, and this is real, Red. The poachers are armed, and they don't care about shooting people." Cameron picked up her hand and held it firmly in his. She felt warm and helpless at the touch of his hand. Although helplessness was exactly the opposite of what she wanted to feel.

"You came here to help the elephants, not to sign up for a war. That's what this is Mac. It's a war. You could die out there."

"I understand that you mean well, Cameron, and I get that I'm not a soldier like you ... but I want to do this. I've been following this herd for months. They're my family. Men, vicious and brutal men, are going to try to kill them, and I can't let that happen."

Mac looked into Cameron's eyes and noticed they were more green than blue today. "With you as our eyes from the air, we'll have an advantage. So, you'll kind of be there."

Cameron let out a heavy breath. He drew her in and held her, resting his chin on top of her head. Mac wrapped her arms gingerly around his middle, careful not to touch his wound. He was warm. She wanted to look up, only it felt like one of those kissable moments, and she didn't want to deal with right now.

She gave him a light squeeze. He let out a soft groan.

"I'm so sorry. I didn't mean to hurt you."

"Don't worry about it. Didn't hurt that much."

"Liar." Mac stood then grabbed her hat. "Let's do this." She said the phrase energetically, trying to hide the real fear she had about tonight.

He smiled and held out his fist. Mac fist-bumped him. Then swiftly headed to the door. She could hear the bed frame squeak as Cameron rose and followed close behind her. Though she was scared, she also felt strong. Maybe it was the rifle that made her feel like a bad ass. Maybe it was her love for the elephants. Maybe it was both.

"Will you take care of Fenny if something happens to me?"

Cameron stopped; his brow furrowed as he crossed his arms. "Don't talk like that." As if in agreement, Fenny paused from eating his cricket to look back at the pair.

"I'm just being realistic."

"No, you're being stupid. Fenny will be waiting here for you to come back, and I don't want a dog. Now let's go check on supplies."

"Fox," she corrected, "I'm just saying ... I haven't talked to my mom or planned out anything."

"Worry about that the next time. You're going to be fine, Mac."

She stopped at the door and turned. "How could you know?"

"I'm not going to let anything happen to you. You just worry about aiming, and I've got your back."

Chapter 48: Fly, My Pretty

Two green trucks were parked outside the armory. Cameron arrived, Mac riding shotgun. He waved to Thato who was loading the back of a truck with water. Thato returned a two fingered salute.

"Looks like the gang's all here." Mac pointed to the other rangers while Cameron parked. They walked to a large table with hard platted tactical vests and ammunition boxes. Abebe, Bandile and Roshan were loading guns. The men looked solemn. No one spoke; only greeted the pair with slight smiles.

Mac started to put on a vest. The weight was uncomfortable. She wondered if the others would be uncomfortable with a woman on the team.

She released the empty mag from her rifle and took the three other magazines out of her pouch. Bandile pushed a green metal ammo box over to her as Thato joined them.

"We don't have enough to fill all those." Bandile's chubby face filled with an infectious smile. "Maybe one."

Mac chuckled. "I guess I'm a little overzealous."

"Just aim good," Roshan added, "and you won't need so many."

They all laughed. Mac knew then the all-male group had accepted her.

"Hey, friend." Cameron walked up to Abebe. "Are we good to go?"

"Yes, Kendalie should join us shortly," Abebe replied.

"That's good. He'll be a real asset." Cameron patted Abebe on the back, then continued walking. He looked over his shoulder, as he headed to the storage facility. "I'm going to get Beetlejuice."

Abebe put his rifle on the table and started cleaning it. Without looking up he said, "We know the other side is armed. Don't anyone hesitate if you get an opportunity for a shot. They will not."

Silence blanketed the small group. Abebe moved by Mac. "He worries about you. I don't."

"Oh, really?"

"Because anyone with hair that red has the devil on her side." He let out a deep laugh. "Besides, I've seen you shoot. You're good. Just don't get in the way of any of their bullets."

"That's my plan." Mac tried to sound confident. *Well, this is what you came for. To make a difference.*

Cameron returned with a black bag slung across his chest. Kendalie had joined him and was carrying the drone's storage case.

"I don't think you should be carrying anything," Mac scolded Cameron. "Your stitches."

"I told him that myself," Kendalie added. "He is very stubborn."

Grimacing, Cameron set the bag down. "I'm using my good side, and it's not heavy."

"Tell that to your face." She pointed to the bag, "What's in it?"

Cameron reached into the bag and pulled out radios, microphone clips, and earpieces. He handed five sets to Kendalie who took one, then passed the rest to Abebe, Bandile, Roshan, and Thato. Cameron walked over to Mac with hers.

"I'll be with you," he said softly while looking into her eyes. "You must trust me and do whatever I tell you. No going rogue. This is my area of expertise."

When she took the radio set, he brushed his hand over hers.

"I know and I will." Mac slid the radio in a pouch attached to her belt. She ran the microphone wire under her armor then clipped it to her collar. She then stuck the small earpiece in her ear.

"Okay, Abebe," Cameron said, "you, Bandile and Thato are team Gold. Kendalie … you Roshan and Red are team Blue."

Cameron paused, looking as if he was going to say something, then he took off Mac's hat and tousled her hair.

"Hey! What was that for?" She grabbed the hat and pulled it down on her head.

"For good luck, Red." He winked then walked over to help Kendalie.

"Argh. You're such a pest." Mac turned. Abebe, Bandile, Thato, and Roshan were standing in front of her with goofy looks on their faces. "What?" Unexpectedly, Bandile took her hat, and they all playfully ruffled her hair.

"We all need luck." Bandile grinned. Mac couldn't help but laugh. Laughing felt good.

243

"Ready?" asked Kendalie, his composure more serious.

"Almost," Cameron responded as he was assembling the drone. He put on gloves then took small bags out from the black pouch he carried and carefully attached them to Beetlejuice.

"What are those?" Thato reached to touch one of the small bags.

"Be careful," Cameron said. "You don't want to accidentally get any of the dust on you and then rub your eyes. These are spicy little gifts for our poacher friends. After one of these things drops, if you see a cloud of dust, avoid it, unless you like pepper spray." Thato backed away.

"Okay, it's ready." Cameron headed to the control room. "Stay clear. I'm going to go start it up."

Mac picked up her rifle, ensured her safety lever was in position, then clicked the loaded magazine into place. Kendalie joined them and loaded his gun.

"Testing … testing," Cameron's voice came through Mac's earpiece.

"I hear you," Mac answered, followed by a verbal confirmation from each person in the group.

"Good, comms work." Cameron's voice was loud in her ears. "You guys go. I'm going to verify the herd's location then see if I can locate any uninvited guests. We'll need to get into position as soon as possible. If they get too close, we'll lose an elephant tonight."

"Load up," Abebe said.

Grabbing the handle of the truck door, Mac paused. This is one of those times. This is where one decision, one moment in time that you can never take back, changes your life forever. Mac recalled how Keene died. How if he hadn't gone to Clay Jones's ranch, he'd still be alive. I could be making the same mistake. Then she remembered his passion for animals and keeping them safe, his love for, and his dream to come to Africa. She thought of the elephants and how they cared for their young, mourned their dead, and deserved a life free from poaching.

Mac's heart swelled with conviction and a trust that wherever Keene was, he was going to protect her. She opened the door and stepped inside.

Chapter 49: Take Out the Trash

Chen entered the restaurant. Standing in a small alley, Gacoki watched, his broken body aching. His right eye was still swollen shut, though he could see Chen clearly through the lens of hatred from his other eye. The smaller bodyguard walked in with Chen. The larger man took out a cigarette, lit it, then leaned against the door.

Gacoki knew the disadvantages he had, that if he was smart, he should wait a few months, get stronger, then make his move. But he was afraid Chen might not stick around with all the attention the last shipment had caused. It was now or never, Gacoki decided. He had no faith the authorities would find Chen, let alone connect him to the ivory poaching.

Besides, the authorities would want to send Chen to trial, and he would do ten years, at most. That wouldn't be good enough. It wouldn't be justice for Gacoki's father.

Removing a bottle of acetaminophen from his pocket that he had stolen from the hospital, Gacoki shook three pills out, popped them in his mouth, then chewed them. The sour taste caused his mouth to salivate as he swallowed the chalky pieces.

I need to do this quickly and quietly. The fat man will be the hardest. I'll need to lure him out without raising the alarm. They'll all pay for how they tortured me.

He walked back along the alley then looked down the main street. He noticed a shop filled with clothing and went in. Taking the opportunity when the storekeeper was distracted, he picked up a woman's kaftan and scarf then slipped quickly out of the store.

Once back in the alley, he pulled on the long, flowy dress and draped the scarf around his head, nose, and mouth. He ran his fingers along the handle of a scalpel, another souvenir from the hospital. He concealed it within one of the long sleeves, as he walked toward the restaurant, he picked up a discarded basket from the trash and whatever he could find to make it look like he had items for purchase.

Bai was still at the door. His cigarette smoked down to the filter.

Holding the basket in front of his face, Gacoki came out of the alley. Bai's flicked the cigarette butt to the side as he looked at him.

Gacoki waivered his walk, as if struggling with the weight of the basket, then crumpled to his side. He lay still, listening for footsteps.

"Hey." Bai yelled. Gacoki didn't move.

"You need to leave here." The light click-clack of dress shoes approaching.

"Hey, you." Footsteps stopped. A sharp pain stabbed at his side as he felt a shoe nudge him.

"You need to move, lady."

It took all his self-control to not flinch or cry out. *Come just a bit closer you oversized idiot.*

Bai nudged him a little harder; he still didn't move. The large man grunted. Gacoki felt a hand on his shoulder pull to roll him over.

Quickly, cut him deep.

247

Gacoki withdrew the scalpel from his sleeve, then plunged it up into Bai's neck, just below his right ear. With all his force, he dragged the blade across Bai's neck, deepening the blade as he went.

A vertical red stream flowed from Bai's neck. He had made his mark, severing the carotid artery. Gacoki kicked up, pushing Bai backward. Bai's eyes stared with wide disbelief.

A wicked smile grew across Gacoki's bruised face as recognition shown in Bai's eyes. He leapt onto Bai's large chest and raised the blade again. Bai grabbed his bleeding throat with one hand and threw Gacoki off with the other. Pain shot threw him. He stifled a scream as his battered body hit the ground, tearing at his already injured flesh. White dots flashed across his vision as Gacoki fought to stay conscious.

Bai struggled to his feet, then staggered toward the restaurant's door. Gacoki shook his head, trying to clear it, then stumbled after the big man. He tackled Bai to his knees, but Bai continued to crawl. Before he could get far, Gacoki jumped on his back, grabbed his thick black hair with one hand, and pulled Bai's head sharply back. Bai's neck exposed, Gacoki drew the scalpel across, this time hitting the left artery. Bai gargled as he began to aspirate from the blood flowing into the airway.

Though the man was still alive, he was losing consciousness fast. Gacoki rolled off him. Cursing his own pain, he slowly dragged the giant toward the alley. By the time they reached the shadows, Bai was dead. He patted him down and came across the grip of a handgun. Checking the magazine, he smiled. God is guiding me now. *Fully loaded. But I only need two bullets.*

Gacoki threw trash over Bai, then checked the doorway. No one had come by. Turning to look, he mused at the fitting end. Trash. *That's exactly where you belong.*

Crossing the parking lot, he passed the bloodstain. *Hard to miss if someone comes through here. I must act quickly.*

Chapter 50: Bumpy Ride

Mac felt as if she had been riding a mechanical bull for the last hour. She gripped the metal frame of the truck to keep herself from being bucked into the dense vegetation as Roshan navigated the truck over the bumpy terrain. She glanced behind her. Kendalie seemed unbothered by the jostling and dips.

"It's not the time for migration," Mac shouted over the grind of the engine. "The herd shouldn't be more than a few miles from the last time we saw them."

She stared into the distance, looking for any signs of them. The new moon gave them little light to see; the darkness providing an advantage for escape to the poachers.

"Herd is only a mile north," Cameron said through the earpiece. "In a clearing. They are stationary … over."

"Any reason?" Roshan asked over the grind of the truck's motor.

Mac gave a worried look to Kendalie. After hundreds of years of being hunted by man, elephants have changed their habits. Instead of traveling during the day, they rest.

"This is unusual," she said. "Something might be wrong."

Kendalie nodded.

"The herd is circling a single elephant," Cameron responded. "It looks like it is time … they're making a protective wall. Over."

Mac's stomach sank in a nervous drop that had nothing to do with the terrain. "The elephants will surround the mother to protect her and the baby. The poachers will have no trouble shooting one, if not several of them before the herd will run, possibly trampling the newborn." Her blood boiled at the idea that poachers had no mercy and would happily take advantage of this very private and precious moment. "We have to keep them safe!"

"We will," Abebe's voice answered in her earpiece. "We'll get as close as we safely can without alerting them, hide the vehicles in nearby trees or tall grass, then wait."

Cameron's voice came over the radio, "Hurry, they're almost there."

Chapter 51: One Down, Two to Go

The Chinese Restaurant's hallway seemed longer to Gacoki than the first time he met with Chen. A red curtain divided the restaurant from the toilets. Meat, garlic, and the umami fragrance of soy sauce filled the air. His stomach rolled, then cramped with hunger as he slowly approached the curtain. The clanging of the pans in the kitchen and tinny sounds of the music being pumped through the speakers covered any little noise he might make.

With the fat one dead, I need to watch out for the sneaky little one.

He reached the end of the hallway, tilted his head so he was using his good eye, then peeked through a small opening between the curtain and the wall. On the far left of the room, there was a man with two prostitutes, judging by the way they dressed and fawned over the man twice their age. Chen sat at a table talking on his cell phone. Jiang stoically stood guard.

The wait staff paced between the two tables. He gripped the gun, his finger lining the slide as his other hand wrapped around the grip. He carefully slid his finger on the trigger. *Take out the bodyguard. No hesitation.* Leaning against the wall, Gacoki took a slow, deep breath, envisioning what he would do. The pills must have started to work, or maybe it was adrenaline as he felt little pain from his broken ribs now.

He wondered if the other man at the far side had a gun and if he would interfere, protect his whores.

Even if he did, the man wouldn't be able to draw before his mission was complete.

I could just shoot Chen from the safety of this curtain ... though that would rob me of the expression on his face when he realizes the man he left for dead would be his judge and jury.

Heat rose in his face. He didn't know if it was nerves or a fever coming on. Maybe it was both. All the staff was in kitchen. It was just Chen, Jiang, and the threesome in the room.

Now!

Gacoki slid through the curtain, gun first, pulling the trigger.

Jiang was quick and reached for his gun, but Gacoki had the element of surprise on his side and fired before he could grasp it. Jiang stared with a look of surprise as blood poured from the hole between his eyes. He collapsed like a puppet whose strings had been cut.

One of the women screamed. Chen stared in disbelief; the phone held frozen to his ear.

"End your call ... *Chen*," Gacoki spit out his name. He addressed the threesome at the far table, "If you don't move, I won't shoot you."

The man at the table raised his empty hands in surrender. "Not looking for trouble," he answered in an American southern drawl.

The staff made no attempt to intervene. He didn't know if they'd called the police or escaped. Either way, he had only minutes if he wanted to get away.

"We can make a deal," Chen stated. "I can forgive your failure and the money you lost me."

"You're an arrogant bastard."

"You still pissed about your old man? He knew the risks." Chen still had one hand on his cell phone, "You want money?"

Gacoki noticed Chen's other hand slowly move.

"Put your other hand up!"

"Screw you." Chen tilted his chin up, then moved quickly.

Gacoki reflexively stepped right, as his brain registered the *pop* of the gun. Glass shattered behind him.

Gacoki pulled the trigger twice. Crimson blossomed on Chen's stark white shirt. Chen looked down at his chest then stared sharply at Gacoki.

"Now your debt is paid, *Dragon*."

Chen gurgled blood in reply before the life in his eyes faded to emptiness.

Gacoki's shoulders slumped in relief and exhaustion. He quickly looked over at the threesome.

"I didn't see anything," the man said, his arms around his whores. One had her face buried in his chest. The other stared at Chen, her hands covering her mouth. No sounds came from the kitchen.

Gacoki's shoulders relaxed as he realized it was finally over. He calmly turned and walked out. The sun was directly above him cutting through the clouds in a kaleidoscope of sunbeams, as if God himself was parting the clouds in celebration of ridding the world of an evil man. He could almost hear angels singing. He felt lighter; anew.

"I can finally live!" he declared to the heavens then disappeared into the crowded streets of Mombasa.

Chapter 52: Poacher's Snare

Orange, red, and purple colors blanketed the sky as the light started to fade to black. The churring sound of the fiery-necked nightjar and the rolling whistle of the African scops owl seemed to surround them. Under it all, low guttural growls and snorts of the herd confirmed they were close.

"See anything, Cameron?" Mac asked.

"Affirmative," he responded. "Hold on—" After a painful silence, Cameron said, "Thermal imaging shows three on foot, from the south … closer to team Gold. Gold, you have about three minutes. Two on foot approaching from the east … closer to team Blue … Blue, you may have five minutes. Over."

Roshan, Kendalie, and Mac jumped out of the truck and quickly grabbed their rifles. Roshan parked to the west of the herd and Abebe reported he parked to the east.

This is real, Mac thought. *We are in danger. The herd is in danger. It's time to fight.*

"Move closer to the herd, Blue Team," Abebe commanded Mac's team. "Try to hide in the grass. We don't want to startle the elephants … they may trample the calf if it's been born. Over."

"Team Gold, there are rocks south of the herd," Cameron said. "They will probably use them for cover. Get on the other side of those. Stop them before they reach target. Over."

"Copy," Abebe responded.

The light had faded to almost complete darkness. Fear crept through Mac's mind as well as anticipation and excitement.

Roshan, being more familiar with the area, took the lead, followed by Mac, then Kendalie. Roshan was fast and Mac had to push herself to keep up.

Mac kept on Roshan's heels, stumbling at times, but managing to stay upright. The thick grass hit her pants and would have cut her legs like blades had it not been for the thick fabric's protection. The three of them covered half a mile of rough terrain in four minutes. Mac's heart was racing to the point she felt dizzy, yet her senses seemed to have sharpened. The sounds of the cicadas were deafening in the quiet. As they neared the herd, the crunch of the grass and rumbles from the elephants seemed to be all around her.

Roshan held up a closed hand. Mac stopped. Kendalie's footfalls behind her ceased. The three of them listened until Roshan opened his hand flat and gave a forward motion.

The elephants' vocals turned longer and louder, like thunder. A dust cloud from their stomping blew over them and Mac stifled a cough as they reached the edge of the vegetation cover. They were much closer to the elephants than Mac assumed they would be. It didn't give them much wiggle room. She felt like she could reach out and touch their legs.

"The herd seems … agitated," Mac spoke quietly into her mic.

Roshan knelt quickly and Mac did the same. He pointed up ahead and slightly right. After her eyes adjusted, she could see Roshan was motioning to the small set of rocks Cameron mentioned during the briefing. The three of them ran in and crouched behind them.

"We are to wait here," Roshan said.

"Blue Team …," Cameron's voice "… you should have a visual on your targets. Over."

"See'em," Roshan answered, then pointed. Mac followed his finger and could see moving shadows.

"I'm going around," Kendalie stated. I will try to get them from behind." Then added, "Don't shoot me." He rushed past Mac and Roshan then disappeared into the night.

Roshan tapped Mac on the shoulder and pointed at the elephants. Mac felt her stomach drop.

"Proceed with caution," she told the group. "Amahle is baring down, about to give birth. We don't want to spook them."

Cameron's voice, "We'll do our best, Red. Gold, do you have a visual?"

"We don't have a visual," Abebe's voice sounded over the radio.

"Targets are at the site," Cameron said. "Gold … enemy at your six o'clock. Ready to drop the payload to flush them out—be prepared to go in. Over."

"Do it," Abebe responded.

Within seconds, three *thud-puffs* sounded followed by a dark cloud in the area south of Mac. Coughs and curses cut through the night, as well as the strong scent of pepper. Mac was thankful she wasn't downwind.

"Bulls-eye," Cameron exclaimed.

A single shot broke the night. Mac jumped. Then another.

Trumpets of warning filled the night. The elephants tightened their defense around Amahle, then turned to face out, toward the noise. The elephants threw dust in the air with their trunks, rocking back and forth as if ready for war. Fear grasped Mac. She was close, very close to thousands of pounds of angry elephants.

"One shot, one on the ground ... think he is surrendering ... one ran off," Abebe declared. "Bandile followed. Over."

"I see them," Cameron responded. "They are headed north, around the east side of the herd. Over."

"Look." Roshan tapped Mac on the shoulder then pointed up, slightly right of the first man she could see. "See the other ... he is crouched down."

Mac quickly noticed the other man and nodded.

There was yelling, then another shot. The poacher that was not crouched ran towards the tall grass.

"Stay and cover the herd," Roshan said to Mac. "I am going after the runner. Cameron, one headed west. I'll need help locating him in the grass. Over."

"Got your six," Cameron responded.

"Two are being secured," Thato said.

"Thato, go cover Mac," Cameron ordered.

"Copy," Thato responded.

"Cameron, give me a location of the runner, this is Bandile."

"He's right in your path. Proceed with caution. Looks like someone is behind him."

"That is me," Kendalie's voice was a whisper.

In the dark and with the multiple conversations in her earpiece, Mac was getting confused on where the rangers were located. The grass seemed to rustle all around her and random shouts from men filled the night. She couldn't tell who they were or where they were coming from.

Not knowing what to do, Mac returned her focus to the elephants. She spotted the man Roshan had pointed out to her. This time she could make out the shape of a gun raised and pointed in the direction of the herd. Without hesitation, she raised her gun and focused on the man's chest.

The elephants rocked back and forth and called out their warnings. None were running. They were standing their ground and protecting their family.

"Red! Your one o'clock. He's too close to the herd. Take the shot."

"I have him," Mac stated. She steadied her rifle. The man was well within position to kill Adia, one of the younger females. Anger rose within her as she remembered the elephant they found butchered just days ago.

"Take the shot, Mac," Cameron quietly said. "Before he does."

Mac focused on his chest. Her heart pounded. She was about to shoot a person—kill a living being.

This isn't right. But I can't let him hurt the elephants.

She took a deep breath—a bead of sweat rolled down her cheek. '*Take the shot before he does*,' Cameron's words echoed in her head—she held her breath as she slowly applied pressure to the trigger.

Adia is going to die if I don't shoot.

She quickly shifted her aim down and squeezed the trigger.

The *pop* of the rifle was followed by the man's screams. She had made her mark, striking his upper thigh. He dropped his rifle and crumpled to the ground. Mac started toward him.

"Red, stop!" Cameron yelled in her earpiece.

She immediately stopped and crouched down out of instinct. One of the elephants, Shunga she thought, must have had heard the scream. The matriarch of the group was approaching fast. Her ears were pinned back, head and trunk lowered. She was running towards the man on the ground. The man must have seen her as Mac could see him scrambling away, reaching for his dropped gun. He picked up his rifle and pointed towards Shunga—he was too late.

A horrifying scream hung in the air as Shunga trampled the man. Mac watched in horror as Shunga turned and went back to him. She stood over him and lifted a mighty foot. The man held up his hands in a useless attempt to protect himself, his gun now lost. He screamed again, followed by an audible *crunch* as Shunga's foot stomped to the ground.

Shunga touched the now silent man with her trunk, then stepped on him again, as if to make sure he was dead. All Mac could see now was the man's arm, bent unnaturally upward, unmoving. Seemingly satisfied she had neutralized the threat, Shunga returned to the circle of elephants.

"I'm going in," Mac whispered, her voice shaky. "I'm going to see if he's alive."

"Just leave him," Cameron ordered. "Even if he's alive, there's nothing you can—Mac! Incoming on your left."

Mac broke into a sprint, running towards the rocks and the dead man.

"I've got your back." Roshan's voice.

She could hear the ground under her feet and someone behind her. Then she was airborne.

What the …?

"*Omph!*" Pain ran up her knee as she slid across hard dirt ground. She quickly turned and realized she had tripped over a rock.

"Red? Red? Are you okay?" Cameron's voice was laced with panic. "You've stopped moving."

A shadow came out of the night. She tried to grab for her gun, only it was missing. Her gut clenched in fear. *Oh no! I must have lost it during the fall.*

She looked frantically to her left and right for the gun. *It's too dark!* Mac's hands blindly felt across the hard ground as a figure quickly approached. *He's got a gun!* She raised her hands defensively. *I'm going to die.*

A shot ripped through the air. Mac flinched and unconsciously felt her body for blood. Then two more shots fired. The man jerked, then turned and ran.

"I can't see him," Roshan exclaimed as he ran into Mac's view. "He ran into the brush."

"Got him," Cameron stated. "He's heading north. I don't think he's coming back."

Mac closed her eyes tight as she exhaled a long breath she didn't know she had been holding.

"Red? Are you okay?" Cameron's voice was calmer now.

"I'm ... I'm ... I'm good thanks to Roshan."

Roshan smiled and held out a hand to pull her up. She took it. Once up, she could see the black shape of a gun on the ground. The elephants were all turned into the circle now and she was safe to retrieve it. As she grabbed for it, she almost tripped again, over the dead man that Shunga had trampled.

He was stamped into the dirt with his chest flattened inward. His face turned to the side, mouth open, in a frozen state of terror. Mac could see a dark wet looking patch in front of his mouth, she held back vomit as she realized that must be the man's insides, forced out from the weight of Shunga. A bone poked through the flesh of one of his legs.

Mac quickly turned her head, thankful of the dark night for sparing her the gross details.

"He's dead," Roshan said. "Let's go."

"Mac, I'm on your left," Abebe said then came into her view. "Kendalie, copy?"

"I see Thato with the two captures, Kendalie and Bandile are close ... there is someone on the ground."

"Bandile, copy?" Abebe said.

The conversations over the radio were dizzying in Mac's ears again. A sense of disorientation overcame her as she forced herself to concentrate on Abebe's voice. It was like playing a live action video game without a monitor.

Bandile spoke breathlessly, the crunch of grass and footsteps echoing in the mic. "Copy. I see ... I see ... oh no."

"Stop and surrender ... put it down now!" Kendalie yelled.

"I said put it down ... hands up!"

"No!" Bandile shouted. "Wait!"

Pop. Pop.

"What? What is it?" Abebe looked in the direction of the shots. Mac didn't know who said what or who fired.

"Bad ... it's really bad," Bandile answered. "Kendalie shot him ... it's really bad. You need to come here. Over."

"I'm headed to you," Abebe responded. "Cameron, are we good?"

"All clear."

Mac looked over at the circle of elephants. Through the sea of legs, she could see a calf. The calf was slick, wet, and trying to stand, though failing comically at it.

With death comes birth.

The larger females kept their wall of protection, while the younger ones and Amahle tenderly nudged the calf with their trunks and feet. They knew that the sooner it stood, the safer it would be.

"The baby is okay," she whispered as she felt her own tears roll down her face. The joy and awe at what she had witnessed overwhelmed her and she forgot about the battle that had taken place outside the elephant circle. She forgot she was alone. She assumed Abebe and Roshan had left to assist Bandile.

"You did good, Mac," Cameron said. "Now get out of —Mac. Do. Not. Move. You have a visitor behind you. Turn slowly."

Mac's body begin to shake as she turned to meet Shunga, the matriarch and recent poacher killer. The elephant was within a meter of her. Mac's breath caught in her lungs.

Shunga turned her huge head so one of her eyes met both of Mac's. Mac could make out her thick black lashes, even in the low light of new moon.

I'm going to die.

Neither moved. Mac noticed secretions, resembling tears, streaming down the big mammal's face. This was a sign of celebration. Celebration of the new calf. Shunga didn't move closer, simply raised her truck and sniffed Mac. Gently touching her pants, jacket, then knocking off her hat. Mac giggled as Shunga ruffled her hair with her trunk. Her warm breath blowing in her face.

She remembers who I am.

Shunga trumpeted, then turned back to join the herd in celebration.

"You're welcome," Mac whispered.

Chapter 53: Last Man Not Standing

There was a knock at Mac's door. She had been in her quarter just long enough to shower.

"Just a minute," she called out as she grabbed a long t-shirt and shorts.

"They picked up the two poachers. They are waiting until the morning to get the third."

"Hoping the elephants move away?"

"Safer if they do … plus more light." He nervously shifted from one foot to the other.

"And the man that was shot … was it really—" Mac looked at Cameron.

"Yes. It was Siyabonga. Kendalie shot him. He didn't know who he was, but he was going to poach from our own herd." Cameron placed a hand on Mac's shoulder, "I won't pretend to understand why ... I just know sometimes they get tangled into these things."

"I am so sorry." She shook her head. "I know he was one of your men and you knew him for such a long time."

"He wasn't on our side last night—can I come in?"

Mac moved from the doorway. Cameron walked in and sat on her bed.

"You, okay?" His voice was gentle. Mac knew that he wasn't just referring to Siyabonga's death. He was also referring to the poacher she had killed … or helped kill.

"It was my shot that dropped him. Shunga finished the job, but I basically killed him."

"Don't feel bad for him," Cameron stated.

"How can I not feel bad?" Mac's voice cracked. "A person died because of me." She sat beside Cameron; he enveloped her in his arms.

"More than fifty rangers were killed by poachers over the past year. They didn't care about those rangers." He pulled her in close, "You did good, Red. You should be proud. You saved our family, our elephants."

"I know I had to do it, but I will never forget how he looked. What if he was a father?" Mac pictured hungry children and meager means, like the children she saw at the medical tents.

"Red—" Cameron lightly touched a finger under her chin turning her face to meet his, then bent over so they were nose to nose, eye to eye. "I want you to listen. I'm going to tell you it's not your fault and you are going to have to believe me. People who poach animals are criminals. They made the choice to be there, at that time. They knew the risks. That is not your fault. You did your job."

"But—"

"You didn't even kill him. Shunga did. Do you understand, Red? You must think of it that way, or it will consume you."

"I understand."

The image of the man raising his gun at Adia, filled her thoughts. She cringed at the notion of what might have happened if they had arrived five minutes later.

"Good." Cameron kept his face close; his eyes focused on hers. "Because I want you to be proud that you protected lives today, the lives of innocent creatures that deserve to live just as much as anything else on this planet."

She could feel his warm breath and the intensity of his words through his gaze. Yes, she had done well. She had protected the herd. Mac nodded her head, letting Cameron know she understood.

"Was Jacob with any of them?" she asked.

"Abebe and the others said they didn't see him." Cameron sat back saying, "They were all well-armed, but no sign of him."

"I didn't see him either." Cameron seemed relieved. "Do you think he had a change of heart?"

"We can only hope," he sighed.

"There's a brand-new elephant in the world." Mac placed her hands on her hips and stifled a yawn.

"Yes, there is." Cameron ruffled her hair.

"Are you ever going to stop that?" Mac asked. The grin on his face confirmed there was no chance of it.

Cameron stood, as if to leave. "You should get some sleep, Red."

Mac's energy was starting to wane and sleep sounded good, though she didn't know if she could manage it.

Mac glanced out her window at the sliver of moon in the night sky. Images of the events passed in her mind. She visualized the herd touching and nudging the calf and celebrating the life that had just entered the world. The pleasant image was replaced with the man's mangled body. She could still hear his screams from when Shunga had trampled him.

"Cameron?" Mac's voice was barely a whisper. He turned and looked at her. "Would you please stay with me tonight? I don't want to be alone. I just want to sleep, but I don't think I can … I just—"

"Of course." He opened his arms and Mac ran into them, trembling, then started to cry.

Chapter 54: The Morning After

Dark dreams faded as Mac slowly became aware of the rise and fall of Cameron's chest under her head. They were both drenched in sweat, but she didn't move. She felt safer than she had felt in a long time. Once she moved, this moment ... this perfect moment ... would be gone forever.

"Are you awake?" Cameron spoke softly.

Mac considered feigning sleep; instead, she answered, "Barely."

"Did you sleep well?"

"I must have. I don't remember anything." Mac looked up to face him. "Thank you for staying."

"No worries."

She lay her head back on his chest. Cameron drew her in as he placed a long and gentle kiss on the top of her head. The two of them barely fit on the single bed.

"Red?"

"Yeah?"

"I don't want you to take this wrong—"

Mac's stomach tightened. The words after a phrase like that were never good. She rolled back so she could look him in the eyes.

"I think you should go back home."

Anger and hurt rose through a part of her like magma pushing through fissures in the earth—ready to explode—while another part of her felt relief.

Her brow furrowed. "Do you think I can't handle this?"

"Red, I do want you here."

"Then why ask me to go?"

"Because ... because I love you." Cameron squeezed her firmly.

"You love me?" Mac couldn't form those same words and give them back.

"Yes, and I don't want to be the reason you get hurt, or you stop being you. You are a kind and gentle person and this place—this job—it's none of those things and it will harden you. And when it does, it will be all my fault ... and I can't live with that."

Mac knew Cameron was right about the job, but at the same time, he assumed all her choices had been because of him. And though she did love him in a way; there was something missing. Something she had with Keene.

"Cameron, I—"

He stroked her hair. "You don't have to say it back or not say it. I just wanted you to know."

She tempered her anger and her ego. Cameron was talking from his heart and saying what she had been feeling for the last week, that this wasn't what she wanted to do. She had just wanted to say it first.

"First, my decisions have been my own. So, you're giving yourself too much credit. Second, Keene and I dreamed about having a sanctuary together. We were going to come to Africa ... save elephants. After he died, the dream didn't feel right anymore. I came here to honor him. I came here hoping ... well, I don't know what I was hoping for ... happiness maybe." Mac sat up. "I want to move on. It hurts too much to live the life Keene and I wanted without him. I need to figure out what *I* want to do."

"I'm not asking you to leave tomorrow," he said gently as he tucked a piece of her hair behind her ear.

"I'm not leaving because you asked me to."

"I should never have let you go last night." Cameron's eyes seemed to focus on hers, as if searching them for forgiveness. "What happened last night was my fault. How it will change you is my fault."

"I don't think I gave you a choice," she replied.

Cameron pulled her back down to him and held her for several minutes longer. "I ... if you would have died—"

"Don't worry. You wouldn't have suffered long; my mom would have killed you." Cameron chuckled and minutes passed as she listened to his heartbeat, feeling the slow rise and fall of his chest. "I'll stay another few weeks to make sure the new baby is healthy. Besides, I want to make sure that village gets their bees."

"By the way," he said, "what do you want to call the new baby elephant?"

"I get to name him?"

"Yep, I cleared it with Chimp months ago."

"I know it isn't African, but I want to name him Keene."

"Keene is a good name." Cameron paused. "Ready to go see him?"

"Yes." Mac jumped up. Goosebumps rose where the cooler air hit her hot skin. "Let's go see baby and mama!"

Chapter 55: Home

Mac walked out of Chimp's office and headed to her quarters. It had been two weeks after the baby elephant, Keene, was born and she was ready to go home.

"Hey!" Cameron jogged up to Mac. "You excited? All packed?"

"Yep. Just going to get my bags."

"I heard Kendalie came through and was able to deliver the bees and volunteers from that nonprofit."

"Yes. And they kept their promise about waiting. No elephants were harmed, and the village is starting to make money off the honey ... thank goodness."

"Well, that was all you, Red," Cameron said, tipping his hat back. His blonde sweaty hair stuck to his forehead.

"Let me help you with your bags and Fenny."

***

Within minutes, Cameron pulled the truck up to the airstrip. Standing in front of the plane was Abebe, Bandile, Roshan, Thato, Lebron, Corinne, and even Bruce.

"What's all this?" Mac asked as they pulled up.

"Well, we couldn't let you go without saying goodbye."

Abebe walked up and opened Mac's door for her, helping her out. "Many blessings," he said and unexpectedly hugged Mac. "Be safe and may the sun always smile on you."

"Thank you, Abebe. I will miss you," her voice wavered, overwhelmed by the show of affection.

"Here, Miss Mac." Lebron stuck out his hand. Dangling from it was a necklace made of braided dark brown strips of leather with an elephant shaped wooden charm hanging from the middle. "I made this for you … so you don't forget us."

Mac took the necklace and placed it around her neck. She had packed the silver chain with the ring Keene had given her. It felt like it was time.

"It's beautiful, Lebron, and I could never forget you." Lebron grasped her tightly. "Fenny is going to miss you too." Hearing his name, the fox's nails scraped the plastic carrier as he let out a small anxious yip. Lebron ran over to see him off.

Bandile, Roshan, and Thato walked over and gave her a group hug, then took turns ruffling her red hair. Mac didn't complain this time. "You guys are the best; I won't miss you messing with my hair, but I'll miss all of you."

"Make way, make way." Corinne squeezed through the group of men and handed Mac a paper sack. "Just some food to get you by, if Bruce's flying doesn't make you throw up."

"Hey!" Bruce called out from the plane as he and Cameron loaded Mac's luggage and Fenny's crate. "I'm not that bad."

Chimp's Jeep rolled up to the group. He slowly got out from the passenger side and Rachelle jumped from the driver's side.

"Mac." Chimp held out his thin arms. "We will indeed miss you."

Mac went to him and embraced him gently; she was sad to think that this was the last time she would see him.

"Thank you again for your wonderful suggestion for my home." Chimp gestured to Rachelle, "I will hopefully get to see it full of children soon."

"Yes, thank you, Mac." Rachelle wrapped Mac in a long embrace. "I was so grateful when Chimp asked me if I'd like to run a pediatrician's office out of his home … and that it was all your idea." Tears traveled down Rachelle's face. "It's more than I could have asked for."

"And now there isn't logistics standing in the way." Rachelle blushed.

Cameron jogged up to the group. "Your flight is about ready to board," he said, picking her up in a big bear hug. "I'm going to miss you, Red."

"I'm going to miss you too," she whispered into his ear. "Don't be stupid and let her go again."

Cameron set her down gently, then looked up at Rachelle and smiled.

"I won't, Red."

"You guys are good together." He nodded, then let her go.

"Oh, Jacob called me," Cameron said excitedly.

"What? You're kidding me. What did he want?"

"He wants a job."

"And you are seriously going to give him one? You trust him?"

"With the Golden Dragon and his bodyguards dead, he's a free man. He wants to change. He's going to help me with the ranch. I could use his help."

Mac still didn't feel the same about Jacob as Cameron, only that was his burden, not hers.

"I hope it works out." And she meant it. Cameron smiled. Mac was going to miss that smile. And although she didn't love him, like she had loved Keene, she still loved him.

"Okay, Red. Let's get you on that plane so you can go make the world better. I'll protect our herd, so don't worry about them. And I'll send you pictures and updates on baby Keene."

Cameron gave her another hug and kissed her cheek.

"Thanks, Cameron. Please take care." Mac turned to face the plane as a boxer would face her opponent. "Let's go, Bruce, before I change my mind about flying with you." Bruce gave her a silly salute and cheesy grin.

Once on board, she settled into the front seat beside Bruce.

"Looking forward to home?" Bruce asked as he started the engine.

"Yes—not the flying part. Once I get to Mombasa, I have to catch a flight to Germany then to Washington, DC before finally reaching San Antonio, Texas. It is going to be a long couple of days."

"Well, here we go." Bruce pushed in the throttle and the plane moved forward.

Gazing out the window, Mac observed all her African friends gathered, waving at her. Tears started to roll down her cheeks as she waved back at them. The rangers were waving and jumping up and down, which made her laugh. Corinne blew her a kiss and Mac blew a kiss right back. Chimp stood smiling, covering his eyes from the sun as Cameron and Rachelle stood close to each other, both with a hand raised, open palmed. Mac put her open palm on the window in return. It was a short time in Africa, but she felt like she was leaving family.

"Hold on to your seats, ladies and Fenny," Bruce instructed as the plane started to roll faster. "Time to get you home."

After a few moments of unpleasant bumpiness, the sensation of being lifted and flying smoothly through the air felt sweet and freeing. As the plane headed east, the elephant herd came into view. She could see baby Keene, standing between Shunga and Amahle, healthy and happy.

Mac tightly grasped the wooden elephant, on the necklace Lebron gave her and pictured Keene. A part of her life was being left behind. And that was okay. She didn't know why, but she finally felt at peace with his passing now. It was as if his spirit was born again in that baby elephant, and she could move on. Africa had healed her heart.

She was glad she had traveled to Africa and lived part of their dream. She would always love Keene, and no one could replace the love they had. But now ... now it was time to live her life.